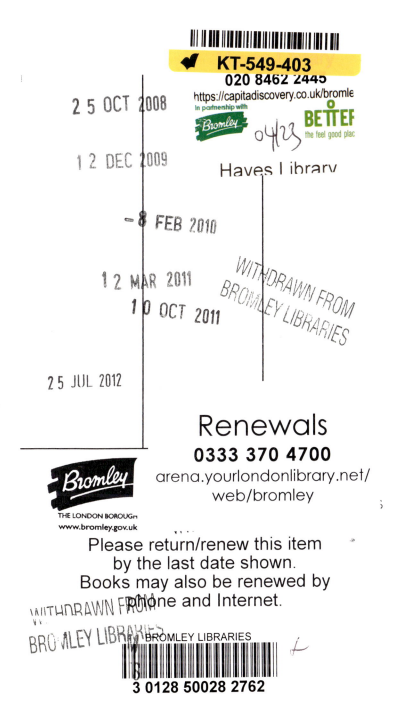

KT-549-403

020 8462 2445

https://capitadiscovery.co.uk/bromle

In partnership with

Bromley

04/23

BETTER
the feel good place

Hayes Library

Renewals
0333 370 4700
arena.yourlondonlibrary.net/
web/bromley

Bromley

THE LONDON BOROUGH
www.bromley.gov.uk

Please return/renew this item
by the last date shown.
Books may also be renewed by
phone and Internet.

Gold for Durango

James Buckley Armstrong is on his way to see about the missing owner of a small newspaper when he comes upon a young woman fighting off two men. The deadly use of his .44 Colt has just changed the men's attitude when her husband rides up. His first words, pointing to Buck, are 'Hang him.'

Narrowly escaping the necktie party, Buck runs headlong into a range war and a series of gold bullion robberies. With a third shipment ready to leave the mines, Buck comes up with a plan. At a fork in the trail, though, the mine owner's agent begins to wonder how far to trust Buck. Others are also wondering about Buck. Among them are the town's most influential banker and the local vigilante committee.

Gold for Durango

Carlton Youngblood

A Black Horse Western

ROBERT HALE · LONDON

Typeset by
Derek Doyle & Associates, Shaw Heath
Printed and bound in Great Britain by
Antony Rowe Limited, Wiltshire

CHAPTER 1

Buck pulled the black stud horse to a halt, not positive of what he had heard. He'd been dozing in the saddle and wasn't sure he'd actually heard anything. Sitting loosely in the saddle on top of the little rise, he turned his head slowly one way and then the other, listening. Nothing.

The horse, taking advantage of the stop, let his head drop toward a clump of cheatgrass and pulled a mouthful.

'Well, horse, I guess I was dreaming,' the big cowboy muttered. Over the years he'd come to trust the ugly black horse. More than once the animal had seen or heard something Buck had missed and with a twitch of its ears had given warning. Not this time, though. Nodding, the rider stuck a heel in the horse's side.

'Come on, fella, just cause I'm asleep doesn't mean we can just sit here doing nothing. We've got a job to do.' The horse was used to the man on its back talking to himself and, as usual, didn't twitch an ear in response.

The horse hadn't taken two steps, though, before its head came up. Both heard the scream this time. A woman's scream, coming somewhere off to the left, down in the tree and brush-covered bottom of the shallow ravine. Reining in that direction, Buck loosened the thong holding the Colt Dragoon in his holster.

Not knowing what he'd be coming into, the cowboy held the black to a walk as he rode through the stand of cottonwood trees. A thin, shallow creek could be seen through the underbrush as it wound its way along the ravine bottom. Seeing a flash of movement ahead, Buck eased himself out of the saddle and, ground-hitching the horse, slowly made his way forward.

A big man, measuring a little more than six feet tall with the wide square shoulders and a chest that tapered down to a narrow waist typical of a horseman, he somehow didn't look comfortable out of the saddle. After hanging his flat-crowned Stetson from his saddle horn, his scarred boots with rundown heels made little noise as he moved through the trees.

'No,' he heard the woman yell, her word choked off abruptly. A man laughed.

Easing around a straggly pine tree, Buck stopped, knowing his trail-worn denim pants and faded red shirt would blend into the shadows. Three people were in the camp, the remains of the breakfast fire smouldering in the centre of the small clearing. A big man standing off to one side near a jumble of blankets from someone's bedroll, watched as a smaller, thin man struggled with a woman. The men were, from their worn dusty pants and faded shirts, someone's hired hands. Scuffed high-heeled boots and worn floppy, wide-brimmed hats told the story – a pair of out-of-work cowboys, probably riding the grub line.

A big toothy smile spread across the weasely face of the man holding both the woman's hands in one of his as he pawed at her shirtfront with the other, ripping the material. The woman, dressed in a split riding skirt and white ruffled-fronted shirt, fought back, trying to kick at him while twisting away. The big man watching from a short distance away stood with his hands hanging empty at his side, an empty smile fixed on his face.

'You wanted this, missy,' the thin man sneered, 'can't tell me you didn't. Now you can yell all you want, there ain't nobody gonna hear. Hell, you might as well just relax and enjoy it.'

'No,' the woman screamed again, kicking at his shins only to have him push her off balance. The thin-faced man let her loose as she fell, landing on her back in the dirt.

Buck figured he'd seen enough and stepped from behind the tree as the man reached for her arm.

'Now,' Buck said, his right hand resting on the butt of his Colt and his voice carrying clearly across the camp, 'that isn't exactly true. There is someone listening and I don't think treating a lady like that is going to cut it.'

'Where in the hell did you come from?' the thin man snarled, stepping back and letting his hand fall near the six-gun holstered on his thigh. The big man standing across the way didn't take his eyes off the fallen woman; his smile remained set. 'Don't you go messing in something you don't know anything about, cowboy,' the weasel-faced man snarled.

'Well, I don't see how that's possible,' Buck said, standing relaxed and ready. 'The woman said no and I think she means it. So, no it is. Now why don't you just step away and let her up.' Buck watched the man but let his eyes keep tabs on both the woman and the big man, too. For a long moment, nobody moved.

The woman was the first to react, coming quickly to her feet and scrambling away from her tormentor.

'Carl,' the thin man, not taking his eyes off Buck, called out, 'don't let her get away.'

Buck saw from the corner of his eye the big man start to move toward the still cowering woman. Quickly flipping his Colt free of the holster, and without aiming, he put a bullet in the dirt near the big man's feet. The man stopped. At the same instant the smaller of the two grabbed for his revolver and had it half out of the leather when Buck's next shot took him in the chest.

The big man's body jerked as if he'd been the one taking the .44 slug. Buck, still holding his smoking gun ready, watched as the smile left the man's face.

'You . . . you killed him.' The words came hesitantly. 'You shot him. You didn't need to do that.' Slowly, as if trying to understand, the man turned to face Buck, his voice rising. 'He was all I had and you . . . you shot him. He's dead.'

The last words were bellowed out as he thrust out

8

his big hands reaching for Buck as he came charging across the clearing, running right through the smouldering camp-fire. The girl screamed. Buck frowned as he thumbed back the hammer and shot the big man twice in the chest.

For a few minutes all was still. Faintly, Buck could hear the woman's sobs, looking he saw her standing frozen, one hand holding the ripped shirt together. The two dead men lay where they had fallen. Somewhere across the creek Buck heard a bird, its call sounding tentatively.

'Are you all right, ma'am?' he called softly to the woman.

'Yes, I think so,' she whispered tentatively. 'You killed them.'

'Yeah, I did.' Buck replaced the spent rounds and shoved his Colt back in the holster. 'Now, you'd probably feel better if you wrapped yourself in one of those blankets there.'

The woman nodded and started to move toward the nearest bedroll only to stop at the sound of horses breaking through the brush. Before he could move, Buck found himself surrounded by half-a-dozen mounted men, all holding rifles and all watching him with expressionless stares.

'Mr Ludel,' he heard the woman say. None of the men responded or even looked in her direction.

The men were all working cowboys with the exception of one, obviously the leader. That man, after a brief glance at the woman, reined his roan horse around and trained his eyes on Buck. While the others wore their denim pants stuffed into the tops of their shotgun boots, this man's wool pants hung straight over the boot tops. Dusty Stetsons shaded the faces of the riders, but Ludel's hat was a narrow-brimmed felt and looked fairly new. For a long moment nobody spoke, the only movement the tail of one or another horse as it brushed at a fly. Finally, the leader, not taking his eyes off Buck, spoke.

'Hang him.'

CHAPTER 2

'You can't,' the woman yelled out, panic filling her voice. 'He saved me. You can't hang him. It wasn't him that brought me here. He saved me.'

Buck kept his eyes on the leader. That was where the order would come from and that was where his first bullet would go. Facing men who held their rifles with such familiarity meant at his first move he'd be shot to pieces, but in that instant Buck knew he'd get at least one. That man knew it, too.

'He had nothing to do with it, Mr Ludel,' the woman went on, her voice losing its pleading tone. 'It was those two. I don't know this man, but he saved me and you can't kill him for that.'

Another long moment went by with nobody moving. Then, with a flip of his head, Ludel nodded and reined his horse around.

'Cover yourself, woman. Reynaldo, get her horse,' he ordered.

A swarthy-faced man sitting to one side of the leader swung out of the saddle and stomped through the trees, reappearing in a few minutes leading a

11

saddled black and white pinto. He stood holding the horse's headstall while the woman, clutching a dirty woollen blanket tightly around her shoulders, put one foot in the stirrup and used the other hand to pull herself into the saddle. Ludel nodded again and, without glancing at either of the dead men or Buck, spurred his roan back the way they had come with the woman falling in behind. The other riders followed leaving Buck and Reynaldo in the clearing. Reynaldo stuck a boot into the stirrup and swung up.

'I will tell you, *señor*. That is Señor Rufus Ludel,' Reynaldo said, his voice soft and the Mexican accent cutting his words short. 'He owns the Crown ranch. The woman is Mrs Ludel. The two men you killed used to work for Crown. Señor Ludel is an important man in this part of the country and I think it would be a good thing if you were to just keep riding until you are a long time away from here. *Comprende señor?*'

Buck let his body start to relax. He hadn't been aware of how tense he'd become and it felt good to loosen up a bit.

'Yeah. Well, I understand that Mrs Ludel won the day and saved me from a hanging. I don't understand much more than that, though.'

Reynaldo took the makings from a shirt pocket and, after rolling a smoke, tossed the papers and tobacco sack to Buck. 'You don't have to understand. Señora Ludel saved you. If Señor Ludel had said hang you, you would now be dangling from that tree. That's all you have to understand.'

Buck quickly rolled a quirly and tossed the tobacco back. Striking a sulphur match, he put fire to his cigarette. It was hard to judge what kind of man this rider was, sitting his saddle slouched and comfortable. The saddle itself told something about him, though. Unlike the usual hulk owned by a rider, this one had a high cantle to give the Mexican's lower back support. Typical of the *vaqueros* of south Texas, the horn was as big around as a man's upper arm and stood high above the rider's thighs. Wide stirrup leathers hung low indicating Reynaldo was a tall man. Silver conchos and decorative tooling embellished the dark brown leather of the saddle. This was a very expensive piece of work and told Buck he was talking to a proud man. A tall, proud man who wore his revolver on his left side, the butt of the pistol facing forward.

For a time neither man spoke. Finally pinching the fire from his smoke, Reynaldo nodded and, pulling his horse close, swung up into the saddle.

'It would be best, *señor*, for you to continue riding on your way, *comprende?*' Touching a finger to the broad brim of his hat in a short salute he kneed his horse and disappeared into the trees.

Buck watched him go and then hunkered down with his back to a tree. For a while he sat there, smoking and thinking about what had happened. Looking across at the two bodies he shook his head.

'Well, boys, if it weren't for you lying there so peacefully, I'd almost say none of this happened. Now what do you suppose that was all about?'

Dropping his cigarette into the remains of the fire, he toed dirt over the smouldering sticks. 'And I wonder what my new friend, Reynaldo, is going to say when he finds out I have business in this part of the country. Seems likely he'll find out. I do hope the idea of stringing me up is forgotten by then.'

Searching through the pockets of the two men he'd shot and wrapping their meager belongings in a neck scarf, and after making sure the camp-fire was out, Buck got on his black horse and followed the trail through the brush left by the Ludel crowd. At least, he thought, they seemed to be going the same way.

Since leaving the Green River country, Buck had been taking his time travelling south towards Silverton. The telegraph message sent by Professor Fish had caught up with him in Leadville and brought an end to his relaxation. Until the interruption, for days on end he'd been riding the back country, stopping whenever he found a likely looking stream for a little trout fishing. There were more than a few days he'd decided for no reason not to saddle up and ride, simply lazing away the day sitting and, well, relaxing. Prof Fish's telegram changed all that.

'Well, horse, guess it's time to put away the fishing pole and go see what's got the good professor all excited about.' Like most solitary men, Buck had gotten into the habit of talking to his horse during long periods of time spent away from people. As usual the black stud paid no attention.

Tightening the saddle cinches, Buck slapped the black rump before swinging into the saddle. 'It'll do both of us some good, I reckon. You've had it so easy lately, getting all fat and sassy.'

The trip south toward Silverton meant crossing the San Juan Mountains over the Stony Pass. From the directions he been given, the wagon road over the pass was best travelled by horseback. More than once he had stopped to peer down steep embankments at the remnants of wagons that hadn't made it. Marks cut into trees showed where block and tackle had been cinched to the trees so wagons could be let down. By the time they had reached the flatlands south of the mountain range, the black horse had had every ounce of fat ridden off him.

Buck stayed on the trail through the brush left by the Ludels and their men until it climbed out of the ravine. Where the rancher had turned west, Buck and the black horse continued on south, riding into Silverton late in the afternoon.

Silverton was a bustling town. Although it hadn't rained in a while, the main street was hock deep in a morass of mud, churned up by heavy wagon traffic. Like a magnet pulling at a knife blade Buck's eyes were drawn toward one sign hanging over the boardwalk. The sign simply read SALOON.

Dropping the reins over the hitch rail in front, Buck stood for a moment and then, nodding in silent agreement with himself, took the neckerchief from his saddle-bags. Asking directions, he walked down the street to the sheriff's office.

' 'Morning,' Buck was greeted as he stepped out of the sun. When his gaze adjusted to the darkened room he nodded his response.

'You'd be the sheriff?'

'Naw, jest a deputy. Hell, fer that matter, I guess I ain't no more than a jailer, 'cept there ain't nobody back there in the jail.'

'Well' – Buck stepped to the desk the jailer was sitting behind and dropped the knotted neckerchief on to the desk top – 'I got here the belongings of a coupla men I left a few miles north of town. There isn't much, but I thought I'd bring in what they had. Maybe someone could tell who they were and tell their people where to find them.'

From the weak sunlight that streamed through a dirty window, Buck saw the jailer's head was nearly hairless. His ears stuck out at almost right angles to his head, a band of grey hair circling above them. The rest of his head was smooth pink skin. The man's eyes, deep sunk tiny black beads and almost hidden in dough-ball cheeks, stared unblinking at Buck.

'What do ya mean, ya brought in their belongings? What was wrong with them coming in themselves?'

'They're dead.' Uninvited, Buck hooked a chair with one toe and sat down.

Pawing through the few items Buck had taken from the two men, the jailer stopped and looked up.

'You got any idea who these men were?' Buck shook his head. 'Waal, can you describe them?'

'Yeah, one called the other Carl. He was a big man. I got the idea he was a slow thinker. The other one, his partner, was a smallish man, thin-faced and had a sneaky look to him.'

'Carl, huh. Yeah, that'd probably be Big Carl and if the other one was skinny, then it'd be Hugo. They're some kind of cousins. See one, you'll see the other. Now, what happened that you brought in their stuff?'

'Well, *they* couldn't.' Thinking he'd got the bad news out of the way, Buck went on, 'I shot them.' He almost smiled at the look on the jailer's face at that.

'You shot them? Waal, I guess this is something Sheriff Brickey should know about.'

Buck smiled and stood up. 'Yeah, that's what I thought. Tell you what, I just rode in and am dry all the way down. You go get your sheriff and I'll take care of my horse. Tell him I'll be standing at the bar over in the saloon.' Not waiting for a reaction, he walked back out into the sunshine.

Leading the black down the street, he turned in at the livery stable. Typical of stables everywhere, rows of stalls lined the broad passageway from the wide double doors back to the doors at the back. Stacks of baled hay filled space behind the stalls.

'It'll cost ya two bits fer a stall and another two bits for grain,' the old man said, as he stepped out of the tiny office to one side of the doors. 'Or you can put yer horse back in the corral out back. There's hay and water; cost you two bits.'

Buck laughed. 'This is one mean horse, mister. He don't like anyone but me and then most times he doesn't like me much neither. It'd probably be best if he was left alone and the corral sounds just about right. Is there a place to store my saddle for a day or two?'

'Yeah, you can hang it in there,' the old man said, pointing at the office, 'nobody'll bother it.'

Taking a few coins from a pocket, he handed them

over and stripped the leather off the horse before leading the animal to the back.

'Now, horse,' he chuckled as he forked hay into a trough, 'you mind your manners, hear?'

Nodding to the stable-hand, Buck made a beeline for the saloon.

Standing at the bar with a half empty glass of beer in his hand, Buck soon felt at home. Except for a couple men sitting at a table over against one wall, another man leaning against the far end of the bar and the bartender, Buck was about the only customer. The barkeep, after pouring the beer, stayed close by, idly wiping at a glass with a dirt-grey bar towel.

'New in town?'

'Yep,' Buck didn't want to encourage the man.

'Well, this is the place to be, all right, the Gold Dust Saloon. Doesn't look like it, I suppose, but there's a lot of business done in this town.' The bartender was obviously lonely.

Buck nodded. 'I noticed the street out there. Looks like a lot of traffic's keeping the mud from setting up.'

'Ah, that mud is because the city fathers decided to wet the street a few times a day. Keeps the dust down, ya know. With all the wagonloads coming down from the mines, that damn dust would just bury the town if the water wagon didn't come through every so often.'

'Wagons from the mines, huh?'

'Yeah. Old Charlie Baker was a smart one. He found the first bit of gold and staked his claim.

Trouble was, he staked the wrong place. His claim was over south of town a mite. The real gold comes from the mines up in the hills on the other side of town. But the old man was lucky. He built his stamping mill before his gold vein ran out. Now his operation is kept busy milling the ore from the mines that're producing. The old man died a few years ago and his son runs things.'

'Good for the son, I suppose.'

'Yeah, he's a sharpie, he is. He's made his pa's stamping mill into quite a profitable enterprise. There's talk that he's even trying to get the Denver and Rio Grande Railroad to run a spur line this way. The nearest railhead now is down south to Durango, and that's close to fifty miles away. 'Course, that's only a rumour. Ain't nobody sure it'll ever happen. Be good for everyone if it did, especially young Charlie Baker.' The bartender stopped when someone came though the swinging doors. 'Well, good afternoon, Sheriff. Ain't your usual time of day to be coming in, is it?'

'Nope, Henry, it isn't. I'm looking for a stranger,' the newcomer said, keeping his eyes on Buck, who was looking at the young woman standing a little behind the lawman. 'Johnny tells me this stranger is bragging about shooting Hugo and Big Carl.'

Stopping a few feet away from Buck, the sheriff pulled his short-barrelled Colt and held it casually at his side. 'You want to take that gun of yours and lay it on the bar? And do it slowly,' he ordered, not taking his eyes away from Buck.

CHAPTER 3

For a moment Buck wasn't sure he had heard the man correctly.

'Wait a minute, Sheriff,' he started to explain, but stopped when the sheriff's Colt came up and centred on the middle button of Buck's shirt. Slowly, as directed, and using only his thumb and forefinger, he lifted the Colt Dragoon and placed it on the mahogany bar.

'Now, can we talk about this?' he asked, keeping his voice calm, conscious of the stillness in the long room. Even the barkeep had stopped moving, simply stood and watched, the towel in one hand and a glass in the other.

'Sure. I expect you've got a different story than what old John gave me, but I don't believe in taking chances.' The sheriff let a small smile flicker across his face but Buck noticed his Colt didn't waver.

'Well, I don't know what your jailer told you, but I do know what I told him. Did he show you the stuff I'd brought in?' The sheriff nodded. 'Well, that's all those two had on them. Not much to show for a couple of lives, but that's the way of it.'

'And you did shoot them, though?' the girl asked. Standing to one side, she had looked Buck up and down, obviously making her mind up about him. 'John was very clear about that. He said you bragged about it.'

Buck chuckled. 'Nope, I can't say I agree with him. I simply told him where the bodies were in case anyone wanted to bring them in. Nothing to brag about, killing a man. Even if they deserve it.'

'Did they deserve it?'

'Ma'am, I don't know what your interest in this is, but yes, I'd say they got what they were asking for.'

'Louise,' the sheriff said, still not taking his eyes off Buck, 'I think I'd better handle this, don't you?' The slight smile softened his words. 'OK, tell us about it, stranger.'

'Name's James Buckley Armstrong, Buck to my friends. The long and short of it was that I came upon their camp this morning. They were in the company of a young woman and weren't treating her very gentlemanly. When I spoke up, the one I'd guess was Hugo, pulled his six-gun and I shot him. The big fella came rushing across at me and I shot him, too.'

'What woman?' the girl asked.

'Louise, let me do the asking. Please?' This time the lawman glanced at her before turning back to Buck. 'What woman?'

'Turns out she's some rancher's wife. Half-a-dozen riders led by a man named Ludel came riding up about then and, well, that's about all.'

'Ludel,' the girl said, frowning. 'Might've known.'

21

The sheriff holstered his pistol and nodded. 'Yeah, that does make some kind of sense. Old John does have a habit of seeing things that aren't there. I apologize, stranger. Pete,' he turned to the bartender, 'let me buy this man a beer.'

If the sheriff was buying him a beer, Buck thought it'd be safe to shove his Colt back into the holster.

'Well, I guess I can write it up anyhow,' the girl said, starting to turn away, 'not that old man Ludel will like it, having his wife's name in the paper.'

Both Buck and the sheriff watched as she walked out, letting the doors swing behind her.

'Who is she?' Buck asked, after nodding his thanks for the glass of beer and taking a sip.

'Louise Clement. She and her brother Lewis own the local newspaper. She was with me when John told me about the shooting and just had to come along. She's a pretty nice person but there are times when that darn newspaper of hers is just too, well, nosy, I'd guess you'd say. By the way, I'm Sheriff Cord Brickey,' he added, sticking his hand out to shake Buck's.

'Lewis and Louise Clement,' Buck mused. 'They're the reason I came to Silverton, Sheriff. I understand that Lewis Clement hasn't been seen lately. I guess she wrote to some people I know and they asked me to look into it, if I happened to be coming this way. I was, so I will.'

'Yeah, I remember her saying something about writing to a family friend, asking for help. I did what I could, but that wasn't much. He just didn't show up one morning and hasn't been seen since. His horse, a pale-coloured dun that's almost old enough to remember the Alamo hasn't been seen either. No note, nothing.'

'How long ago was this?'

'Oh, better'n a month. More like two months, I reckon. Most all those living in the surrounding countryside have come into town one time or another since then and between Louise and her newspaper and me, I'd say most everyone has been asked and all denied seeing any sign of him.'

'Well, it isn't the first time Professor Fish has asked me to do something impossible. Seems the Clement family are good friends of his and he and I, well, I owe him a lot more than I'll ever be able to pay. When he needs something, I just naturally try to help out.'

'That means you'll be around here for a while?'

'Yeah,' Buck said, finishing his beer. 'Guess I'd better find me a hotel room or something. It's been a long day, what with stopping those two from doing what they was up to and then almost getting hanged for it.'

'What's that about?'

Quickly as the two men walked out to stand on the boardwalk, Buck explained about Ludel's order to string him up.

'You know, that old man is something else,' Sheriff Brickey mused, as he stood looking up and down the muddy street. 'His spread covers a lot of territory down to the south of here. Runs nobody knows how many head of beef. He must be more'n fifty years old. Could be even older. He and Kingston came into the country just after old Baker made his gold strike.

Baker dug for gold, Kingston started out selling whiskey from the back of a wagon before opening the bank, and Ludel, well, he started raising cattle. Baker brought his wife and raised a son, but Ludel and Kingston was always batching it, until a couple years ago. Usually when Ludel shipped cattle, he'd go along with the drive over to the railhead. A coupla years ago, when the crew came back, he wasn't with them. The story is that he went on down to St Louis or maybe New Orleans, nobody knows for sure. Anyway, when he came back, he had a young woman with him. Said she was his wife.'

For a few minutes, while a string of high-sided wagons went by, the rumble of the wagons and the noise of the teamsters' yelling silenced the two men. Buck deftly rolled a cigarette and offered the makings to the sheriff, who shook his head.

'Damn, but that gets tiresome. If it isn't the noise, it's the mud. Worse though, I guess, was the dust before they started watering down the street. Anyway, that's who you were dealing with. Old man Ludel doesn't trust anyone around his wife. He rarely even lets her come into town on a Saturday. When he does, he watches her like a hawk.'

Shaking his head, he went on, dropping his voice as if telling a secret. 'A stranger was in town one time and saw her as the Ludel crowd was just riding in. He let out a yell and called her name. "Nellie, girl", he yelled. Everybody on the street heard him. Ludel just turned the buggy they were in around and drove right back out. It was a long time before he brought his young wife into town again.'

Buck smiled and, pinching out the end of his quirly, tossed the soggy paper into the street. 'I guess there's a lot of reasons for that to happen. The West isn't so full up with people that running into someone you know from somewhere else doesn't happen.'

Brickey chuckled. 'Yeah, I guess. Anyhow, that's why the old man almost had you dangling. The story is he's afraid some youngster is going to come along and take his wife away from him. Or someone like that young man will recognize her and tell everyone where she came from.'

'That's only one of the problems a married man has,' Buck smiled, 'except if it's going to happen, the marriage probably isn't all that strong anyhow. There's been a lot of men found a wife in one of the houses of the line and made a good marriage out of it, too. But what do I know, I have yet to be caught.' Glancing over at the other man, he chuckled. 'You married, Sheriff?'

'Nope. I've been thinking about it a little, though. Louise and I were even talking along those lines for a while there. Until her brother disappeared. That stopped everything as far as she's concerned.' Soberly, Sheriff Brickey looked straight at Buck. 'I certainly hope you can come up with something. Not only for his sake, but for mine, too.'

CHAPTER 4

Leaving the sheriff to his work, Buck figured he would have time to talk with Louise Clement before suppertime. If the man Prof Fish wanted him to look for had been missing for a couple of months, he figured there wouldn't be much that could be done. Possibly he'd be able to get on with his fishing.

Finding the newspaper office wasn't difficult. He simply walked down street, careful of the thick mud whenever coming to one of the cross streets, looking the town over. Silverton was a little bigger than most mining towns, with at least three hotels, half-a-dozen saloons and two banks. Buck came upon the newspaper quite by accident.

Walking the broad plank boardwalk built to keep pedestrians out of the thick mud, he was passing an open door when he heard a harsh voice shouting orders.

'I don't give a damn, woman. And I'm not going to give you any more warnings. It isn't doing anyone any good for you to keep reminding people of those hold-ups. Can't you see the harm you're doing to the town? Hell's fire, you're part of the business community, aren't you? You're only hurting yourself with those stories. But if you don't care about your business, least you could do is think about the others. I'm telling you, the businessmen I represent won't put up with it. You had just better remember that you're a woman who's all alone. Anything could happen.'

Buck didn't like the sound of that and looked through the doorway. Louise Clement, a long black apron hanging from her neck and tied tightly around her slim waist stood behind a low counter with hands on her hips, facing a stocky-built man who was very angrily pounding the counter that separated the two.

'Dammit, I'm not going to be telling you again. Leave it alone! Let it die a natural death. There is no indication that the gang is still in the area. Let it go.' His voice was loud and demanding. The kind, Buck thought, who was used to giving orders and not having them contested. Louise Clement, he noticed, didn't look like she was ready to back down. He thought he'd better try to defuse the battle.

'Or else what?' he asked, keeping his voice soft and his word clear. 'If Miss Clement doesn't do what you're yelling about, what? Maybe she isn't as all alone as you make her out to be. No, sir, I'd say she has lots of friends who'll back up her play.'

The man spun around at Buck's words, his hand automatically dropping to sweep back the bottom of his black wool suit coat, but stopping before touching the holstered revolver. Buck stood leaning against the door jamb, his right thumb hooked over the cedar handle of his Colt and watched the other man's face flush with anger.

'Don't you go messing in, cowboy,' the man snarled. 'This isn't any of your affair.'

'Well, now, maybe it is, Miss Clement being a new friend of mine and all. I don't think I can simply stand by and watch a self-important bully give her a hard time. Now if you've said your piece, which everyone on the street's been listening to, then I'd say it was time for you to move on.'

Coming slowly to stand at his full height, and not letting his hand stray away from his own pistol, Buck let the smile leave his face. The man facing him was as broad-shouldered as the tall cowboy but was a good six inches shorter. Stepping aside, Buck nodded his head toward the open door.

'I don't know who you are, cowboy, but take some free advice: keep riding. You won't last long butting in where you're not wanted.'

'That's the second time today I've been told to ride on. Guess your advice is worth just as much as it costs. Miss Clement, should I just go ahead and toss him out into the street?'

Before the woman could answer, the blustering man stomped out, glaring up into Buck's eyes as he passed by. Buck thought he heard Louise Clement chuckle.

'Now you've really done it, stranger. That's old Brass Kingston. He owns the bigger of the two banks and thinks he's the prime rooster in this hen house we all call Silverton. I don't think making him your enemy was a good thing.'

'Well, maybe not. And I might not have stuck my nose in where it probably didn't belong, but his yelling bothered me as I was walking by. Anyway, I was looking for the newspaper office and couldn't very well just stand and wait for him to finish loud-mouthing you, could I?'

This time she did laugh. 'No, and I do thank you. He'd been threatening me for a while and I was getting tired of it. Now, what can I do for you?' She hesitated and then went on, 'You're not here to ask me not to run the story of your shooting Hugo and that big lug that followed him around, are you?'

'Nope. What you write, as long as it's the truth, can't hurt me too much. Unless either of those two gentlemen has a lot of friends, that is.'

'Those two? They don't do much more than draw their pay and drink it up at one of the saloons down on Blair Street. You do know about Blair Street, don't you?'

It was Buck's turn to laugh. 'From the way you turn your nose up at the name of that street, I'd say it's the home of all the sleazy, low-life saloons and gambling halls. This being a mining town, I'd figure there'd have to be a street like that somewhere.'

'Yes, you've got it right. And that's about the only people who know Hugo and Big Carl. Except out at the Ludel ranch. Last I heard they had hired on out at Crown.' She stopped and frowned, thinking for a minute. 'Yeah, that makes a little more sense. You say they were mistreating Ludel's wife, Nellie? Well, now, that takes the cake.'

Buck let a frown grow across his forehead. 'Let me

in on the secret.'

'Oh, there isn't any secret. It's been rumoured that the high and mighty Rufus Ludel was having a hard time keeping his new young wife happy. Stories going around are that she wants to return to wherever she came from, but the old man won't let her out of his sight. It seems likely she got to that idiot Hugo and offered to pay him to take her out to the railhead at Durango or someplace. And it seems to follow then, that he'd take his chance with her, doesn't it? Yes, I wish I could go out and ask some questions. That would be a good story.'

She stopped again and looked across the counter at Buck. 'But that isn't why you wanted to talk to me, is it? What can I do for you, stranger?'

'Well, first off, my name's Buck Armstrong. And you're the person I'm here in Silverton to see. Seems you wrote a letter to Professor Fish. Something about your brother Lewis having gone missing. The professor wired me and asked that I stop by and see what I can find out.'

'Oh, I didn't expect anyone would come. It's been so long I've about given up hope.'

'All I know is what the sheriff told me. He said your brother simply didn't show up one morning. There must be more than that. Is there anything you can tell me?'

'Cord Brickey is a good man and a good sheriff. He doesn't say it, but I know he thinks Lew simply got tired of working here at the newspaper and decided to ride off. That isn't so. Our father was a printer back East. When Mother died he bundled us up and put his press on the back of a wagon and headed West. For most of our childhood we lived in Cheyenne, but when Father heard about the gold rush here in Silverton, he got out the wagon and moved the press. A year after Captain Charles Baker found the first traces of gold, Father had the *Silverton Herald* up and running. Lew and I took over when Father died a year ago. What I'm trying to tell you is that Lew and I were brought up with the newspaper. It isn't something either of us would ever get tired of doing. Lew just wouldn't up and ride off.'

'Did he say anything, the last time you saw him?'

Louise Clement's face seemed to sag as she looked down and slowly shook her head. 'No. Not really.' She was silent for a moment and then looked up. 'Oh, yes. We were arguing. He was angry and stomped out, slamming the door. That was the last time I saw him.'

'What was the fight about?'

'Lew had been writing editorials about how it seemed obvious that the gang that held up the last two gold shipments almost certainly had to have inside help. Lew thought there had to be someone close to the mine owners, someone to inform the outlaws of just when the shipments were to be made. Brass Kingston doesn't agree. All he can see is that making that claim is bad for business. It just makes everyone wonder if they're doing business with a spy. I asked Lew to, well, not be so adamant about it, but my brother is just like our father was. If they saw something they didn't think was right, then stand back. And maybe he was right. The people here in town have it rough enough, and Kingston does seem to take a lot on himself, telling everybody that he speaks for the business community. For some time now, Lew has pointed out that Kingston is too big for his britches and is trying to rule everything in town. I thought Lew was going a little strong and he thought I was just blind to what the banker was up to.' Once again she stopped and looked down at the floor.

'And that's the last thing we said to each other, our arguing. I'll never forgive myself if' Buck was afraid she was going to start crying – 'if he's dead somewhere and that's the last thing we did, was fight.'

She flicked away a tear and shook her head angrily. 'But maybe you can find out what really happened. He lived in the boarding-house down on Edwards Street and I have a small cottage on the street behind here. When he didn't come in the next day, I went down to the boarding-house. The woman who owns it said she hadn't seen Lew at all that morning.'

'Well, I guess that's where I'll start. I'll probably take a room there myself, if they have one.'

'Why are you doing this, helping me find out what happened to my brother?'

Buck smiled as he squared his hat. 'I owe the good professor a lot. When he asks me to help out one of his friends, I can't very well say no.'

'He and my father were good friends, too. I didn't know who else to contact. Cord, uh, Sheriff Brickey, has done all he could and nobody up at the territorial capitol seems to care. Thank you for coming in to try to find out what happened. It's been nearly three months since Lew disappeared and I've come to think he won't be coming back.'

'What do you think happened?'

'There's no way to prove it, but I really think my brother was killed by someone involved with the gold shipments, or maybe someone from that gang of outlaws. The editorials Lew was writing couldn't have made them happy and I firmly believe that's what happened. I'll go further than that. Somehow, I just know Brass Kingston is involved. I know, it isn't likely, him owning the bank and all, but . . .' She let the thought die. Looking up directly into Buck's eyes, her voice grew hard. 'You search all you want, but if you ever find my brother, it'll be his body, and if you discover who killed him, it'll somehow tie in with the gold shipments.

CHAPTER 5

Taking a room at Mrs Ritter's boarding-house got Buck a place to keep his horse, breakfast every morning and, if he was on time, supper every evening. If he missed the supper hour though, he missed out.

Mrs Ritter, a portly woman whose husband had been killed in a mining accident, told the tall cowboy that she expected him to stomp the mud off when coming in the house and to keep his high-heeled boots off the furniture. Buck easily agreed to the rules and paid for a week's stay. He was, the landlady informed him, just in time for supper.

Sitting around the big table with six other guests, he made himself at home to the meatloaf, mashed potatoes and bowls of steamed vegetables. A basket set in the centre of the table held a pile of warm homemade bread and was covered by a bright flowered towel. All the other guests seemed to know each other and, as they ate, they talked quietly about their day.

Thinking about sleeping in a real bed, after bringing his stud horse up from the livery, Buck turned in early. Sleep came easy and the next morning long before the sun came up he was washed and ready for the day. Coming down the stairs from his room, he was a little surprised to find Mrs Ritter already at work in the kitchen. The rest of the house was quiet and, as she poured him a cup of coffee, she told him that breakfast wouldn't be for another little while.

'I have to be up before the chickens to get things going,' she said, as she bustled around the big kitchen. 'My Andrew was an early riser so I'm used to it. Most of my guests work in stores or businesses here in town and like to sleep in, though.'

Leaning against one end of a work counter, Buck asked if he could talk to her about the missing man, Lewis Clement. Mrs Ritter said she didn't mind, but he'd have to talk to her while she worked. Running the boarding-house and feeding the people living there meant she didn't have time to sit and gossip. Buck watched as she poured flour into a huge bowl and began mix bread dough.

'Well, as I say, I don't like to gossip, but if you're to help that Miss Clement then I'll tell you what I can. It isn't much, I'm afraid. I didn't see Mr Clement at all the day he disappeared. To tell the truth,' she said, her hands busy with the flour mixture as she talked, 'I'm not even sure he came in the night before.'

'Miss Clement said she last saw him when he left the office that evening.'

'Oh, he was here for supper. Mr Clement is a thin man but he certainly likes his food. I don't know where he puts it all. Why, I don't think in all the time he lived here, and that's since his pa died, his sister lives in the house the old man died in you know, well, in all that time I don't think young Clement ever missed a supper.'

All Buck could do was smile and let her talk. 'He was here for dinner,' he started, 'but didn't show up for breakfast the next day?'

'No, and that wasn't usual. But I was busy, as there's always something for me to do. Keeping this many people happy is a day-long job, I'll tell you. And if someone causes me any trouble, it's out the door they go. I don't have time for any foolishness.'

'Miss Clement told me she came by looking for her brother later in the day.'

'Yep, she came in while I was setting the dough out to rise, just as I'll do after I finish what I'm doing now. If there is going to be fresh bread for dinner, I have to let the dough rise. This dough will be for biscuits and it doesn't have to rise. Anyway, while that's happening, I clean up and then strip two of the beds and change the linen. That way, everyone's bed gets done at least once a week. And that day was for doing the room next to Mr Clement's. I'd done his bed the day before. So when Miss Clement asked to see his room, I said yes, she could follow along and look while I went on to change the linen in Mr Osgood's bed.'

'And she didn't find anything in his room to explain where he'd gone?'

'Nope,' Mrs Ritter rolled the big ball of dough out on the floured table and started kneading it, stopping to look up at Buck after a moment. 'You know,

36

I thought at the time it was kind of strange.'

'What was strange?'

'When I opened her brother's room for her that day I saw the bed hadn't even been slept in. Oh, Mr Clement was just like every man I ever knew, he didn't make the bed in the morning. No, sir. But he did pull the blankets up, not like some, I'll tell you. Some men simply throw back the blankets when they get up and then at night, just pull them back up over them. My Andrew was like that. I like to have the bed made each morning so when I get in bed at night the blankets are all nice and flat, not wrinkled and tied in knots.'

'And you don't think he'd just got up early and left after pulling his blankets back up.'

'No, they were all nice and tucked in, just like I'd left them the day before when I changed his linen. He hadn't slept in that bed at all.'

Buck asked a few more questions but didn't learn anything else. After assuring Mrs Ritter he'd be in in time for supper, he walked back down the boardwalk to the sheriff's office. So far he hadn't learned much that would help. Nobody had seen the missing man after he had stormed out of the newspaper office and the only suspect, as far as his sister was concerned, was the banker, Brass Kingston.

Sheriff Brickey was going through a pile of wanted posters when Buck pushed open the office door. The jailer Buck had talked to the day before sat in a chair to one side of the sheriff's desk, resting a white coffee mug on his protruding stomach.

' 'Morning, Sheriff,' Buck smiled, and glanced at

the chubby jailer and nodded.

'That's the man, Sheriff. Came in all proud of hisself and telling how he left two bodies out somewhere in the brush.'

'Good morning, Buck,' the lawman greeted Buck, ignoring his jailer. 'You find a place to spend the night?'

'Yeah. I'll be over at Mrs Ritter's place for a few days.' Standing next to the desk and looking down at the round pink face of the jailer, Buck let his smile grow hard. 'What's this I hear around town that you're telling people I was bragging about shooting those two men?'

The man's face lost some of its colour as he found himself unable to look away. Buck saw his pudgy fingers shake, spilling a little coffee on to his clothing.

'You know, I wouldn't like it if I heard that pack of lies again. Now, you might think about that a little because if someone was to call me a liar or a killer, then I'd just have to come talk to you, wouldn't I?' Buck didn't make it a question. 'And the town would then need a new jailer. We wouldn't want that, would we?'

The jailer tried to set the coffee cup on the desk but his trembling fingers spilled most of it on to the floor.

'John,' Sheriff Brickey cut in, keeping a stern look on his face, 'I think you had better get a mop and clean up that mess. Meanwhile I'll take this gentleman for a cup of fresh coffee and try to talk him out of doing anything rash.' Nodding to Buck, Brickey opened the door and, glancing back, let the jailer see his frown.

Walking down the boardwalk, Buck chuckled. 'I guess I shouldn't pick on your hired help like that, but he did deserve it.'

'It'll do him good to get a bit scared. Old John's about the only man in town who'll take the job, so I keep him on. Every so often, though, he forgets and starts to think he's a real deputy. Now, tell me what you've found out about Lewis Clement.'

'Nothing. Only that his sister thinks a local businessman, the banker Brass Kingston in particular, had something to do with his disappearance. And she has come to believe that wherever her brother is, he won't be coming back. She thinks he's dead, although she didn't say it quite like that.'

Brickey nodded as he pushed the door to the hotel restaurant open. 'Yeah, I've got to believe that's the case. But I don't think Kingston had anything to do with it. Why, it's just as likely to be one of the farmers.'

Taking chairs around a table near the windows over looking the street, the two men ordered coffee. After placing his hat on an empty chair, Buck frowned at the lawman. 'She didn't mention any problems with farmers. Or anyone else for that matter.'

'Well, it's those editorials he liked to write. Lewis was a firebrand when he saw something he thought was wrong. First there was some trouble between Ludel out at the Crown and the farmers. See, when Ludel and a coupla others first came into this part of the territory, there wasn't anyone else around. Oh, the miners and the kind of riff-raff that follows a gold strike, but nobody with an idea of building a life here. Ludel put down his markers and claimed a big piece of land south of the river, about a thousand acres, I'd guess. A coupla other ranchers did the same further out a little later. When two farming families arrived a few years ago, they homesteaded a strip of land along the river closer to town. That area was mostly dry wasteland covered with sagebrush. They looked it over and saw something the others had missed. They worked hard, I'll give them that, digging a series of irrigation ditches and turning the land into prime farmland.'

'That should have made the ranchers happy,' Buck said, blowing the steam rising from his coffee. 'Nothing a ranch crew hates more than having to cut winter feed.'

'Yeah, and they did sell a lot of hay and feed to the ranchers and everyone was happy. Until Ludel decided he'd made a mistake when he didn't include that bottomland in his claim. When some of his cattle tore out the farmer's fences, he said it was only natural for the animals to go where the good feed was. If the farmers couldn't protect their crops, he said, then maybe they should sell out and move on. When Lewis learned that Ludel offered the farmers a few hundred dollars he wrote it up making it look like the rancher was trying to force the farmers out. Ludel and the others didn't like that.'

Sipping the hot coffee, the sheriff looked out the window as an ore wagon lumbered past.

'Well, Lewis did write at great length about the problems that the two camps seem to be having. Not so much Garvey and some of the other ranchers, as Ludel out at the Crown ranch. His spread is the closest place to Montague's farm. Rufus Ludel staked out most of the section west of there, everything from the high meadows in the foothills of the San Juan Mountains down to a few miles further on south of town. There're a number of springs up on those flats and it must have looked pretty good.'

'And now Ludel wants the farmers gone so he can lay claim to it?'

'That's the way it looked. For a while. Then he backed off and things settled down. That happened a bit after Rufus brought his new wife to the ranch and personally, I think Old Rufus got too busy trying keep her happy to worry about taking over the farmers' land. But recently he's been at it again.'

'For all that, from what I'm hearing, Ludel then is the only one mad at Lewis Clement?'

'Well, except for one fella in that group of farmers,' the sheriff said hesitantly, frowning a little. 'There it gets a little tricky. You see Elizabeth Montague had been flirting with Clement every chance she got. She's young and pretty and makes no secret that she doesn't want to marry a farmer. Her pa's farm is the biggest, but she wants out. Anyway, she met Lewis at a dance about a year ago. Everybody was there and it was the talk of the town how she hung on him every chance she had. Now that's all right, as far as it goes. But young Royal Balsom didn't like it one little bit. Luke Balsom, Royal's pa, has the other big farm. Royal grew up with Elizabeth and thinks she should marry him. That Royal Balsom is a big young man and can get mean when he's had too much to drink. It was only a few days before Clement disappeared that young Balsom stopped him in the street and knocked him down. There was a lot of yelling and I had to break it up.'

'So you're telling me there are both ranchers and farmers who didn't like Lewis Clement?'

'Yep. If you're looking for people who had something against Lewis, then you can look most anywhere. I'd settle on Royal as quickly as I would Brass Kingston, though. When young people get close to what they think is love, you never know what'll happen.'

'Sounds as if you've had a lot of experience in that field,' Buck said, and watched as the sheriff's face turned red.

CHAPTER 6

'We got us enough trouble around here,' Sheriff Brickey continued, wanting to change the subject, 'without there being a war between the farmers and the cattlemen. Both bring a lot of money to this town and it seems like it'd benefit both to keep the lid on.'

Buck smiled as he put his cup down. 'I have to admit, my meeting with the owner of Crown wasn't very friendly. But he's just like a lot of old-time cattle-men, thinking he's so important that his cattle's cowpats don't stink. My pa was a lot like that. Just knew the cattlemen had all the rights and everybody else could take what was left over. It took a long time for him to admit it was easier to let the farmers grow the hay and sell it to him than for him to fight with the hired hands to do any kind of work that couldn't be done on horseback.'

'Well, that's about the way Ludel and the other big ranchers act, too. 'Course that Ludel has his own troubles.' Brickey smiled and shook his head slowly side-to-side. 'Comes from marrying a younger woman, I expect.'

Buck nodded, thinking back to the anger he'd seen in the rancher's eyes when he ordered the hanging. 'Or maybe,' he smiled, glancing sideways at the sheriff, 'it's just part of being married.'

Brickey frowned and found something out on the street to stare at.

'You say there's enough trouble around here?' Buck asked, thinking he'd probably gone far enough with his teasing. 'What kind of trouble?'

'Well, I don't mean here in town. Things here are real quiet, usually. But there's those gold shipments that were held up not long ago. Happened south of here a ways; shipments from the mines being hit before they get anywhere near the railroad at Durango. There'd been reports of outlaws robbing claims and shipments at the diggings east of here, over at Ophir, but the mine owners here hadn't been bothered until recently. Seems a group of vigilantes formed up over there and hanged a bunch of men. I certainly don't want anything like that to happen here.'

'No,' Buck nodded in agreement, 'I've seen what happens when vigilantes get going. Too many innocent men get painted with the brush and end up dead. If this territory is ever going to become a state, law and order will have to come in legally, not with the help of a mob.'

'Yeah. But try telling that to the mine owners. Every time a shipment of specie goes out, they have to hire a small army to protect it and even that don't always work.'

'Do you think there's anything in what Lewis

Clement wrote about? There being someone here in town in cahoots with the outlaws?'

'I don't know,' Brickey said. 'I know all the shop-keepers and businessmen in town and I certainly don't want to think that one of them could be help-ing that gang out. But,' he hesitated a bit, 'yeah, maybe. Charlie Baker heads up the mine-owner's association and he's pretty smart. He's of a mind that the gang knew more than they should have.'

'What do you mean?'

Sheriff Brickey finished his cup of coffee and pushed the cup away before going on, 'The first load of gold that was lost to the thieves had gone out as secretly as possible. Nobody was supposed to know exactly when it was to be taken out. They loaded up the wagon late at night and had five or six outriders, all armed and ready. There's a place about twenty miles south where the wagon road goes through a narrow stretch of foothills. That's where the gang hit. Shot three of the guards and made off with the gold on pack horses. The second time, Charlie doubled the number of guards protecting the wagon. That time the hold-up was just a little south of Garvey's ranch, out in the open. The outlaws seemed to rise up out of nowhere as the wagon went by. The only survivor said the hold-up men came up out of the brush beside the road as the guards rode by and shot them out of their saddles. The same thing happened to the outriders bringing up the rear. The guards in the wagon were shot before they could react. It was well planned and executed like a military operation. They got away with the gold and didn't lose a man.'

For a minute the two sat looking into their empty cups. 'Sooner or later the governor is going to have to do something, I suppose,' Brickey said dejectedly.

'What about the rumour I hear of a rail line coming this way? Wouldn't that help?'

'Sure it would. That'd be a great boost for everyone. But that'll take a lot of money and so far talk of a spur line is just that, talk.'

Both men looked out the window and watched as a fully loaded ore wagon rolled by.

Getting directions to the Balsom and Montague farms from the sheriff, Buck thought he might start asking question at those places before moving on out to the Crown Ranch. He wasn't sure what he was looking for, but maybe he could learn something by just asking questions about Lewis's going missing.

Balsom's farm was about five miles south-east of town, then Montague's, with the Crown's headquarters a few miles beyond that. He'd be lucky, he thought, to talk to all these folks and get back in time for Mrs Ritter's dinner.

Following the broad wagon road out of town, he held the black horse to a ground-eating lope. Buck enjoyed the crisp morning mountain air. Breathing deep and not pushing the black horse, he soon forgot all thought about getting back to town in time for dinner. Along with the directions, Sheriff Brickey had mentioned something about a couple of the old silver mines located in the hills on either side of the canyon bottom that the road followed. Stopping where Deer Park Creek poured in a series of cascades to let the black drink, he looked up the creek and spotted a mound of tailings showing where, at some time in the past, some hard work had been done.

From the low ridge overlooking the expanse below, Buck could see where water from the river had been diverted to irrigate the various fields. Dropping down off the ridge and on to the flats of the basin, he found himself riding along the San Juan River, a small stream that further north in the mountains of Montana would have been called a creek. Here and there, close to the river-bank, sparse stands of cottonwood and pine trees shaded the surging river. An early spring crop of wheat, their pale green tops bending in the morning breeze moved in smooth undulating waves in the fields. The faint rustling of those waves blended into the constant faint gurgle of the river, making the sound of an unseen bird's song almost seem out of place. Buck was relaxed as he followed the road down and out on to the flatlands. He was simply enjoying the day when he was brought back to earth by a loud order.

'You can stop right there, cowboy. And keep your hands where I can see them.'

Daydreaming as he rode along the river trail, Buck hadn't seen the young man until he came around a small bend. The man stood next to a cottonwood tree with his feet firmly planted, a long-barrelled rifle pointed in Buck's direction.

'Whoa up there, partner,' Buck said, slowly raising one hand while reining the black horse to a halt. 'No need to get all excited, now. And I'd appreciate it if you'd point that weapon somewhere else.'

'I don't reckon I will. It isn't often we catch one of you big cow herders off on his own. It wouldn't be wise to simply point a gun at you and not take the opportunity to pay you back for what you've done to us.'

'Hey, whatever grievance you think you've got, it isn't with me.'

The man laughed and wagged the barrel a little. 'From where I stand, a cowboy is a cowboy. It doesn't seem that any of your kind pick and choose when it comes to beating on us farmers.' His words took on a sneering tone. 'And that's what's going to happen. Now slowly,' he ordered, 'stay on this side and climb down off that horse.'

Buck sat and looked the man over before moving. His sturdy canvas pants and square-toed, thick-soled shoes said he was a farmer. Suntanned, his face was wrinkle free and his full head of hair long overdue for a trimming was blond, sun bleached white where a hat hadn't protected it. Buck figured him to be about 20 or so, full of a young man's certainty. When he jerked the rifle barrel again, Buck nodded and lifted his leg, sliding out of the saddle. The black, freed of its rider, stepped to one side and pulled at a clump of grass.

'Now why don't you just unbuckle that revolver and we'll see just how big and mighty you really are.'

Again Buck didn't move for a minute but studied the man.

'What's your name?'

'That don't matter none. I'm not a cowboy, that's for sure. And that's all you need to know. This time you don't have a lot of help backing up your play, and this time it won't be one of us farmers eating dirt. Now unbuckle that gunbelt.' He chuckled and steadied the rifle at Buck's chest. 'Or would you rather see if you're faster than my trigger finger.'

Standing, Buck saw he was a little taller than the young farmer. Both men were square shouldered, but where Buck's wide chest fell away to his narrow rider's hips, the other's body was one big block. Probably, he thought, a lot more muscle than fat under the sun-faded cotton shirt, too.

'What're you planning on doing, boy?' Buck asked, and saw the farmer's full lips tighten.

'Oh, I ain't gonna sink to your level. No sir. You hang that gunbelt over your saddle horn and I'll put my rifle down and then we'll see. Too long you cattle people have been pushing us farmers around. Well, this time it'll be the other way. Go ahead, unbuckle.' The sneering smile came back. 'Or are you too scared?'

'You sure this is necessary?' Buck asked, and seeing no way out, did as he was told, hanging his holstered Colt over the horn. Slowly he hung his Stetson by its chin strap, too, and taking a pair of thin leather riding gloves from a saddle-bag, pulled them on.

'Oh, afraid you'll get a little dirt on your hands?' the farmer scoffed.

'Nope,' Buck said, and letting his hands drop to his sides, walked straight at the farmer, 'just a little protection for my hands. No reason for me break them up over this.'

49

The young man quickly let the hammer on his rifle down, leaned the weapon against a tree and took a step forward, stopping to meet Buck's approach. Holding his hands up, curled in tight, big-knuckled fists, he waited for the expected attack.

Buck, his hands still hanging loose, stopped a good arm's length away and smiled. 'OK, boy. You got what you wanted. Now what are going to do?'

With a growl of anger the young man threw himself at the big cowboy, looping his right fist in a roundhouse swing. Buck easily ducked under the fist and, sticking his booted foot out, pushed on his attacker's chest, tripping him. Standing back with his hands once again hanging down he waited until the young farmer got up.

'That was crooked,' he muttered, as he brushed the dirt off his hand. Once again with fists up and ready he snarled, 'Come on. No more tricks. Let's see what kind of man you are.'

'Boy, I'm not in this to be fair. Most fights aren't, you know. Now if you don't want to get hurt, I'd recommend you step back a bit and think this over.'

'No, darn it. You're going to get what you deserve,' he yelled, rushing at Buck again. This time wind-milling both his fists, Buck found he couldn't duck fast enough and took a blow to side of his head. Stepping back he felt something turn under his foot and he fell back. Quickly rolling over, he came to his feet, hands up and ready. The farmer stood back, waiting.

'See, take off that gunbelt and without any of your friends, you're not so big an' tough, are you?'

50

'Boy, you've got the wrong ranny. But you're about to make me mad. Now stop it and step away.'

'Hah! You don't even sound so tough now that you've been knocked down. Come on, I'm not finished with you yet.' Fists up with his right sticking almost straight out in front, the young man started forward. Buck waited and watched his eyes. Just as the tow-headed farmer's eyes squinted a little, Buck weaved to his right and then bounced back straight. Thrown off by the movement, the farmer lashed out and missed. Buck brought his right fist across, catching his opponent on the chin. Knocked back, the farmer frowned, shaking his head.

Breathing deep, with his fists once more ready he hunched his shoulders a little and started forward again. This time Buck ducked his body and feigned a motion to the left and came up with his right fist lashing out. The fake confused the farmer and left him wide open. Buck smashed his right deep into the young man's stomach leaving him bent over holding his gut.

Buck waited trying to decide if he should take advantage of the farmer's helplessness.

'That'll be enough,' a voice yelled from somewhere behind him. 'Leave him alone.'

'Boy,' Buck said to himself, 'and I thought I was all alone.' Stepping back and holding his hands out he looked around at the newcomer. The man coming at a clumsy run through the wheat was red-faced from the exertion, his breath coming fast and shallow. Buck waited.

'That'll be enough,' he said again, this time not

yelling. 'There's no need to keep beating on him.'

'Hell's fire, mister. It's this young idiot that wants the fight, not me. Maybe you can talk some sense into his thick skull.'

'Pa, let me take him,' the young farmer growled weakly still trying to catch his breath, holding one hand across his stomach. 'He just tricked me that time.'

'Boy,' the older man said, shaking his head disgustedly, 'can't you see you're on the losing end of this?'

'Why are you on his side, Pa? We got us a cowboy and it's time we taught them they can't just ride all over us.' Glancing to the side he suddenly darted to where his rifle was leaning against the tree.

'No,' the older man yelled, and grabbed the barrel as it was coming around. 'Now, Royal, I said no. Leave go of that weapon, you hear me?'

For a moment the two struggled to take possession of the rifle. Then, giving up, the young man let go and throwing a look filled with hate at Buck, took off running back the way his father had just come. The two men watched as he disappeared in a fold of the field.

Shaking his head and looking a little embarrassed, the older man looked up at Buck. 'I'll apologize for my boy's actions, mister. He, well, we've had some trouble with riders from Crown and Royal is taking it all pretty hard. Once he has time to think about it, he'll be all right, I reckon.'

Turning to Buck he held his hands palms up. 'You gotta admit, it isn't often we see one of you cowboys out riding by yerself. I saw you coming down off that ridge back there and thought about it myself. But Royal there, he grabbed the rifle and took off running. I followed, but I ain't as young as I once was.'

'Why in blue blazes are you two so all fired ready to do me damage? All I'm doing is riding the trail. What did I do, cross too close to your wheat field?'

The man didn't say anything for a minute, not taking his eyes off Buck. 'Well, no. It's just that we haven't gotten along with Ludel and some of the others for sometime. Crown riders have been picking fights with any of us farmers they see and there's been a coupla times when their cattle have gotten into our crops. It's almost like it was a war – Crown against the farmers. There ain't no reason for it either. Why, until recently, Rufus Ludel was buying pretty much all the hay and wheat we could raise. Between him and old man Garvey out at the Rafter G things was pretty good. Now, well, now I just don't know.'

Buck slowly stripped the gloves off, shaking his head. 'Did I hear you call him Royal? Would that be Royal Balsom?'

'Yeah, that's my son, Royal. I'm Luke Balsom. He's really a good boy, this is all just too much, I guess.'

'My name's Buck Armstrong.' Buck didn't offer to shake hands, but simply nodded. 'Miss Clement, from the newspaper in town asked if I could find out what happened to her brother, Lewis. According to Miss Clement, your son and Lewis Clement had some words not long before he disappeared.'

'Royal didn't have anything to do with the

Clement fella getting himself in trouble. My boy wouldn't do anything like that. Yeah, sure, they was yelling at each other there in town one time, but that was settled pretty quick. No, sir. My boy didn't have anything to do with that.'

'Well, it don't look like I'll get to talk with him today anyhow, angry as he is.' Folding the gloves while walking over to take up his horse's reins, he shoved them back in the saddle-bags and wrapped his gunbelt back in place. Settling his hat at the right angle, he stepped into the saddle. 'If you get a chance, I'd appreciate it if you'd explain that I'm not one of Crown's riders and I don't go around waging war on farmers.'

'I'll tell him, fer sure. But he's a little hot-headed at times. I'd probably say now wasn't a good time to try to ask him anything.'

'Yeah,' Buck said, touching the brim of his hat and gigging the black into motion.

CHAPTER 7

According to Sheriff Brickey, Crown headquarters was further on a couple of miles. Riding at a steady pace, Buck didn't let his mind wander. If young Royal Balsom or anyone with a bone to chew wanted a piece of him, he wasn't going to be caught unaware again. Not today, anyhow.

The basin he found himself riding through stretched out before him. Far to the west he could make out the series of basalt bluffs that Sheriff Brickey had said reared almost straight up from the bottomland.

Passing fenced fields of hay, wheat and other crops, and crossing bridges that had been thrown up over irrigation canals, Buck figured the farmers had a good thing going. He had been brought up on a Texas cattle ranch and ranching was all he knew, but it didn't take much to see how things were. If someone could make a good crop of hay, it could hardly help but be profitable. Winter this far north could be long and cold and having a ready supply of hay to purchase made carrying over a herd to fatten up in the spring could mean running two herds to the rail-head at Durango each year.

After a while, the wagon road left the river bottom, veering off to the east. Slowly the road gained in elevation, climbing away from the flats below and the river. Still open prairie, the fenced fields had given way to open range. This was cattle country.

For another hour or so Buck rode, keeping the black at a steady ground-eating pace, not seeing another person. He stopped at a fork in the wagon road, where the main branch contined on and another track, no more than a pair of wheel ruts, turned off to the east. A high arch built from long, tapering, peeled pine logs rose over the ranch track. Hanging from the top of the arch was an iron outline of a crown. This was certainly the way to the Crown ranch headquarters. According to the directions, he should have about a mile to go.

Swinging out of the saddle to let the horse have a breather, he stretched the kinks out of his legs and he studied the countryside. Small clumps of stunted trees, actually no more than tall bushes, broke the monotony of the rolling plains. Far to one side, almost out of sight, a scattering of black specks had to be cattle feeding. Swinging back aboard, he reined the black down the narrow wagon track.

Someone who knew what he was doing had built the main ranch buildings. A huge barn with a full hayloft was the first structure, with a long, low bunkhouse sitting next to it. A couple of outbuild-ings of various sizes, and a series of peeled pole corrals could be seen to one side, extending back behind the barn. All the structures had been placed to block any of the winds that blew out of the north during the long winter months. The road Buck was on ended at the steps to a wide, shaded porch that ran the full length of the two-storey main house. Stopping at the hitch rail, he was about to swing down when he was stopped by an order given from the porch.

'Whatever you come looking for, mister, it ain't here. And you ain't welcome either, so just turn that horse of yourn around and ride out.' The shaded porch was dark and Buck couldn't see who was talking. But from the cold welcome, he figured it was Ludel.

Sitting back in the saddle, and keeping both hands on the horn, Buck nodded.

'Well, that's not the way we welcome riders where I come from. All I want to do is ask a couple of questions,' he said; then talking fast before he could be interrupted, 'Has to do with the departure of Louise Clement's brother, Lewis. The sheriff back in town seemed to think you might have had some idea of what happened to him.'

Ludel seemed to be taller than Buck would have guessed, standing on his own porch than when he last saw him, sitting the back of his horse. The glare at the mounted man was the same, though.

'Stranger, you got your nerve, I'll give you that, coming out here after that set-to we had yesterday. But that don't change anything. You're trespassing on my ranch property. Whatever happened, that blasted Clement had it coming to him, far as I'm concerned. Now, ride on out while you can.'

For a long minute Buck didn't move, then slowly he took the makings from a shirt pocket and proceeded to roll a quirly. Touching a match to the end, he lit it and, as he was about to rein away, another voice snarled from behind him.

'Hey, *señor*, you hear the boss? He does not like to be telling anyone anything twice. Maybe it is a good thing for you to turn around and ride out, *comprende?*'

Using his knees, Buck urged the black around so he could face the man behind him. Reynaldo, standing tall in black charro pants and a high-cut, long-sleeved jacket, his narrow waist circled by a holstered gunbelt, smiled without humour. Buck saw that his right hand was holding a long-barrelled Colt at his side. A floppy, weather-bleached, broad-brimmed hat shaded the man's eyes, but from the way he was standing, Buck didn't think they were friendly.

Glancing back over his shoulder at Ludel, Buck touched the brim of his hat. 'Guess you don't want to tell me anything about Clement's disappearance, so I'll be on my way.' Touching the black stud's flank with a heel, he nodded at the tall Mexican cowboy as he rode past.

Buck didn't look back until he reached the log arch and then turned. Reynaldo had escorted him out and sat comfortably in the saddle holding a rifle pointed at the sky, its butt resting on a thigh.

'Ah, *señor*. Tell me why you did not do as I said and ride on? That Señor Ludel does not like you, I can tell. He has some worry about certain things and you, *señor*, you do not want to let him see you too many times. *Entiendas?'*

Buck lifted a hand and smiled before reining the black away and, setting a comfortable trot, headed back toward town. The afternoon had been pretty much of a waste of time. He'd gotten into a fight and been run off a ranch and nobody had told him anything about what had happened to Lewis Clement.

'Well, one good thing,' he said to the black, 'I should be back in town in time for Mrs Ritter's dinner.'

The wagon road back toward town was as empty of travellers as it had been on the way out. The late afternoon sun was getting close to dropping behind the higher mountains to the west when he saw the black's ears twitch. The horse was not a great beauty, hard-mouthed, strong-willed and pigheaded with a bad temper; it didn't like people and showed only a tolerant respect for the man on its back. The two had been partners for a long time, though, and they got along fine. More than once had it seen or heard something before Buck and, by the ear twitch, he thought this might be one of those times.

Pulling up, he studied the hillside ahead and across the way. Not seeing anything out of place, he was about to poke a heel into the horse's side when he saw the horse look over a shoulder, back the way they had come. Turning to see what was there, something struck his left shoulder knocking him completely out of the saddle. Faintly, as if from far away, he thought he heard the roar of a cannon. He didn't feel it when he hit the ground.

CHAPTER 8

A blunt, aching soreness pushed him unwillingly awake. Fighting to stay in the dark, warm, pain-free depths, the throbbing slowly increased until he could no longer hide from it. Slowly opening his eyes a little, he saw everything in a faint yellow fog. Trying to figure out what was happening, he drifted back toward sleep. It was hard to keep his eyes open and so much better if he just let them close. But the ache was only getting worse. Dull at first but growing rapidly in strength, it seemed to be coming from his hipbones. He had been lying on his side too long causing his hip to hurt. He had to turn over. Unless he moved, the ache deep inside would soon be unbearable. Starting to move, a new, sharp stab of fire across his back froze him in place. Stiff, firm bands had been wrapped tightly around his chest and, as he fell into a deep, dark sleep he wondered if he would ever be able to take a deep breath.

Coming awake sometime later, Buck slowly opened his eyes and remembering, tried not to move. Bit by bit he figured out that he was on his stomach in a bed. Sunshine blasted the far wall, making the large sunflowers of the wallpaper almost glisten. For a while he just lay there trying to remember where he was.

'So, you've finally decided to join us.' The voice was as bright and cheery as the wallpaper. Instinctively, he tried to turn to see who it was. Pain, sharp and cutting speared his back, stopping any movement.

'No, don't try to turn over. You've got a gash on your back that is beginning to scab over and it'll heal quicker if you don't try to move.'

'Who are you?' Buck croaked, his throat dry and crusty like a patch of waterless desert.

'Here, lift your head a little and take a drink of water.' Before his eyes could focus on her, he could smell the clean freshness of the young woman. A sweep of long brown hair spilled over one shoulder as she put a hand under his head and helped support him while he sipped from the glass she held to his lips.

'Now, lie still, Mr Armstrong, and I'll tell you who and what and, as far as I can guess, why. My name is Elizabeth Montague and you are in my bedroom. You've been shot, but you're a very lucky man. Pa thinks you were turning when the back-shooter fired. The bullet struck you at an angle and instead of smashing your shoulder blade, it glanced off. It did damage though, cutting a deep, four-inch furrow. Mother stitched it closed, as much as she could, and you'll have an interesting scar when it heals. Now that's about all I know.'

For a few minutes, Buck lay with his eyes closed, thinking, trying to remember.

'How did I get here? Last I recall I was riding up the wagon road towards town. There was something – I don't remember whether I heard something, or what, but I had stopped and that's all. Something knocked me out of the saddle and I woke up here. In your bedroom.'

Holding the glass to his lips, Elizabeth smiled and raised his head again. The water, cool and almost sweet-tasting filled his mouth. He could almost feel the dry membranes in his throat fill with the moisture.

Elizabeth's smile was full, her teeth made whiter by the smooth suntanned skin of her cheeks. In a world where most women wore broad-billed hats to protect their skin from the sun, it was obvious she didn't bother. Reddish highlights flashed in her rich brown hair as she stood back, placing the glass on a bedside table.

'I'll bet you're hungry. It was yesterday evening when we brought you in and that's almost a full night and day you've been sleeping. Mother thought you'd wake up yelling for food and made a big pot of thick beef stew.' Her laugh was pleasant to hear. 'That's a good sign, you know. If Mother thought you were really in danger she'd be making you chicken soup.' Still smiling over a shoulder, she floated out of the room.

Buck, his face to one side, let his eyes droop closed.

Dozing, he came up from a dream when the woman came back, sitting a bowl on the table next to the water glass. The smell of food reminded his stomach of it having been neglected.

'If we move you very slowly,' another woman's voice said from the other side of the bed, 'and don't make any sudden shifts with your shoulder, you should be able to turn over and sit up.'

Strong hands reached under his chest and lifted his upper body, turning it to one side. Slowly, helping by twisting his lower body, Buck soon found himself half sitting up. The firm arm around him just below the tightly wrapped strip of white linen supported him while Elizabeth fluffed pillows for him to lean against. Settling back, Buck gingerly let his back muscles relax.

Yellow curtains that had been trimmed with white softened late afternoon sunlight streaming through the double windows. Standing beside the bed was a woman, clearly the mother of Elizabeth. The same blue eyes smiled as she waited for assurance that the wounded man was as comfortable as he could be.

'There, now isn't that better? You go ahead and eat as much of that stew as you can. Good beef will thicken your blood and help that wound you got heal quicker, you know.' Just as her daughter had earlier, Mrs Montague smiled at Buck as she left the room.

Elizabeth spread a thick cotton towel over his lap and placed a tray on that. Trying not to spoon the delicious food into his mouth faster than he could chew and swallow, Buck started in. As the level in the bowl went down, and the rush to answer the gnawing of his stomach eased, he remembered something he wanted to ask the young woman. How had she known his name? And how had she come to bring him to her house?

'How did you find me? As I remember, I had passed the last farmer's fence and was up in the foothills, had just left the river.'

Elizabeth's expression stilled. Reaching behind her for a chair, she sat and then stared at her hands folded in her lap.

'I don't know who shot you, but it wasn't Royal Balsom.' She didn't look away from her hands. Buck saw that one was gently washing the long slender tips of the other. Finally looking up, straight into Buck's eyes, she said it again, her words stronger. 'It wasn't Royal, Mr Armstrong. He, well, he does things sometimes without thinking, but he wouldn't shoot anyone in the back. I know he wouldn't.' She let her head drop and stared at her hands again.

'Mother and I were visiting the Balsoms yesterday when Royal came running in with his rifle, all red-faced and angry. He didn't even speak to us, just ran into the house. I heard him stomping up the stairs. A little while later, just as we were leaving, Mr Balsom came into the yard. He explained about Royal attacking you. Mr Armstrong, Royal thought you were one of those riders from Crown that's been causing us so much trouble. He didn't know you were looking for Lewis. Or, I guess he didn't want to know.'

Buck finished the stew and waited. Eventually she

continued with her story. 'Royal came out of the house while we were talking and got all red-faced again when his mother started asking him why he had done what he'd done. He didn't even look our way, just went back into the house. Mother and I came home. After supper, just before dark, Royal came over and asked if he could talk to me. We went out on the porch and he tried to explain. But all the time he was still angry, saying he was right. If he'd beaten you up, he said, at least everyone would know the cattlemen couldn't just push the farmers around.'

Again she hesitated before going on, 'I disagreed and that made him madder. He jumped up and got on the horse he'd been riding. He was shouting at me, telling me I'd see he was right.' She glanced up. 'He yelled that he wasn't giving up. That's the last thing he said as he rode out, that he wouldn't let anyone stop him next time. Oh, Mr Armstrong, I know you think it was Royal who shot you, but it wasn't. It couldn't be.'

Buck wondered. He hadn't given much thought as to who had ambushed him. Actually it could have been Royal or even someone from Ludel's ranch. Reynaldo had followed him out to the arch and was carrying a saddle gun. But then most riders did and somehow he couldn't see Reynaldo shooting someone in the back. If he wanted to shoot you, he'd face you while he did it. And laugh at the same time. He looked up to see Elizabeth watching him, waiting for him to say something.

'I was under the impression you and Lewis '

Clement were getting to be more than friends,' he said finally, 'and that Royal didn't like that. I wanted to ask him about the last time he saw Clement but didn't get the chance.'

'No. Lewis and I, well, we talked a few times when we met in town and he did take me to a Saturday dance once, nothing more than that. Royal didn't like it, though. He likes to talk about us getting married some day, but I don't want to live on a farm. He doesn't understand how that could be, but, well, that's the way it is. Anyway, I don't think Royal would do anything that would hurt anyone, other than trying to beat up on them. He just wouldn't.'

Buck remembered what Sheriff Brickey had said about not knowing what people who think they're in love would do.

'So Royal went storming out, yelling threats. How does that lead you to me?'

'I got my pony and followed him. I was afraid of what he might do and thought maybe I could stop him from acting crazy. But I couldn't catch him. When I heard the gunshot . . . I was sure I was too late. I rode on up the road and saw your black horse just standing there with the reins hanging. You were on the ground and your back was all bloody. You were breathing but I was afraid to move you so I rode back and got Pa. He and Mother helped me move you down here.'

'And you didn't see anyone else? Not on the road or up on the hillside?'

For a moment she seemed to be studying her

hands, folded in her lap. Her voice, when she answered was soft.

'No.' Looking up, her eyes were pleading. 'Please, it couldn't have been Royal.'

CHAPTER 9

Buck rested that night, enjoying the comfort of Elizabeth's down-filled mattress, but after getting dressed, moving as slow and careful as he could, and having breakfast with the family, he said he felt strong enough to ride on into town. Laying around just wasn't easy for him.

Putting his saddle on the black horse was too much, though. When he tried to pick it up he felt the stitches Mrs Montague had put in and had to ask for help. The black didn't like it, and from what Eli Montague, Elizabeth's pa, said, getting the saddle off in the first place hadn't been easy.

'We finally had to wrap a feed sack around his head so he couldn't see us. Blamed fool horse tried to bite and kick anyone who came near him.'

Buck tried not to laugh as he apologized for his horse's behaviour. 'Truth to tell,' he said, trying to make the older man feel better, 'he's not too friendly with anyone but me and sometimes he doesn't like me too much either. But that horse is a good one, just doesn't know the meaning of quit.'

Mrs Montague didn't like the idea of her patient being out of bed and certainly didn't think he should be riding away. When Buck tried to thank her for her doctoring, assuring her he'd take it easy and not tear out the stitches she had sewn in his back, she just handed him a package wrapped in a clean cloth.

'There are a few sandwiches. Good beef and bread I made fresh this morning. Do what I say, now, eat as much beef as you can. You lost some blood and it's got to be replaced.' Buck nodded his agreement. The woman wasn't finished, though.

'Mr Armstrong, I heard you taking to Elizabeth about Mr Clement. You have to understand her. She's not going to marry a farmer. Our daughter made it clear from when she was a little girl that she didn't want to live on a farm. She set her eye on Mr Clement and for a time I thought, well. . . . But that didn't come about. When we heard he had disappeared she had already set her sights on another man, Mr Baker from the stamping mill. Royal Balsom just can't believe her and thinks she'll come around to his way of thinking. But believe me, that won't happen. I thought you should know.'

'Thank you, Mrs Montague. I'm not sure if we'll ever find out what really happened to Lewis Clement, but anything I can learn might help. Thank you for everything.'

The ride back into town was long and tiring. Buck held the black horse to a walk, trying not to jar his back, attempting to keep his muscles loose. His horse didn't like being tight reined, but Buck wasn't

70

putting up with any of his usual behaviour. The sun felt especially good on his back, feeling warm through the faded material of his shirt. Both his shirt and pants had been washed and ironed while he was in bed and he could smell the odor of the soap that had been used. Wrapping the reins around the saddle horn to keep the horse at a steady walk, Buck dozed.

None of the other boarders at Mrs Titter's was around when he slowly pushed open the front door of her house. It had taken a lot out of him to strip the saddle off the black and fork a load of hay to the animal. His movements up the stairs to his room were unhurried and quiet. Stripping off his boots and hanging his hat on the hook on the door, he lay back gingerly, trying to protect his back as much as he could. Closing his eyes he drifted into sleep.

The next morning, getting a pan of hot water and shaving, and putting on his last clean shirt, made him feel almost ready for anything. In time for breakfast, he took an empty chair and took a healthy share of the pan-fried ham slices, scrambled eggs and thick slices of buttered toast. Busy eating, he didn't take part in the table discussions and everyone, after giving him a close inspection, simply ignored him.

Nodding his thanks to the landlady who had sat at one end of the long table, Buck stood for a moment on the porch, adjusting his hat to make sure it was right. He figured he should stop by and tell the sheriff about getting shot. Taking time to tell Louise Clement what little he'd learned would be a good thing, too. Talking to the newspaperwoman could wait, he decided and he walked down the street toward the sheriff's office.

Watchful to keep clear of the mud in the street as much as possible, he crossed over to the sheriff's office and, being careful not to make any sudden moves, climbed the few steps and pushed open the office door. The plump jailer looked up from the ratty newspaper he'd been reading and frowned.

'I figured you'd gone on about your business. Didn't expect you to come barging in.'

'Now John . . . didn't Sheriff Brickey tell me your name was John?' Buck didn't wait for the nod but went on, 'Yeah, John. Anyway, I ask you, is that any way to greet a guest of your fine community?' Buck let a big smile grow hoping the round-faced man wouldn't miss the sarcasm.

'Well, you're here, but it ain't likely you'll stay long.' The jailer's ruddy cheeks ballooned as he smiled. Somehow Buck thought his smile had an unpleasant twist to it.

'Oh? And why should I be leaving? My business in Silverton isn't finished yet.' Toeing a chair back a bit from the desk, Buck sat down, all the time keeping his eyes on the jailer.

John wasn't as nervous as he had been the last time they talked. Buck saw he was enjoying himself and thought his laugh, causing the folds under his chin to jiggle, was almost nasty. 'Whatever business you've got had better get taken care of pretty quick, I'd say. Before the coming Saturday, anyhow.'

'Let's see. By my reckoning, this is, what

Wednesday? Or is it Thursday? Well, it don't matter.' Buck leaned back after making sure the chair's back didn't rub against his wound. He thought he saw a gleam in the other man's eye. 'But you seem to think I should change my mind. Now I wonder why.'

' 'Cause of Reynaldo, that's why.'

'Reynaldo,' Buck said slowly, as if thinking. 'Now where did I hear that name before? Oh, yeah. That's the swaggering Mexican fellow who works for that rancher, the one who lost his wife for a while back there. Ludel, that's the one. But what's he got to do with anything?'

John the jailer was ready and willing to share his news. 'He'll have a lot to do with you, you're still here when the Crown crew comes into town Saturday. He and Mr Ludel were here day before yesterday and when I told Mr Ludel about you shooting two of his men, he got all quiet. Man, I certainly wouldn't want to be in your boots, he catches up with you. No sir. He'll tell that mean-eyed Mexican to take care of you, you can be sure of that.'

'Oh, I bet you enjoyed telling your version of that shooting, didn't you? And you think the loss of those two, Hugo and that big galoot he was with upset the rancher? Seems likely they already knew what happened out there. Don't you recall me telling you how they were part of the gang that came riding in after the shooting was all over?'

'Yeah, that may be. But when I told Mr Ludel you were hanging around, it didn't make him happy.' John was obviously taking great pleasure in his work. 'Made it clear that if you're still around, the next time he sees you, it'll be the last thing you see.'

'Now why would that bother me?'

John's chuckle sounded almost evil. 'Reynaldo's about the meanest man I ever did see. And fast? With that cross-draw of his, he can get a six-gun out better'n anybody I ever saw. It'll be fun watching you back pedal, when he comes in.'

Buck relaxed, stretching his boots out in front of him. 'Didn't you ever notice,' he said pensively, 'there are two kinds of men in this world? There's those who talk a good fight and those who don't waste time talking. Now Reynaldo may be a bad man around those who're easily frightened, such as yourself. That could be. I'd say, from what I can see – and you have to admit there's a lot of you *to* see – that you belong in the first batch ... like to talk but would disappear around the corner before it came to fight. Tell you what,' he held up a hand when the jailer started to interrupt, 'come Saturday, after your hero Reynaldo makes his brag, if he does, I'll come and we'll talk again. Only you better be ready to back up your flannel mouth.'

Sputtering, John came halfway out of the chair, ready to continue the battle when Sheriff Brickey pushed through the door.

'Why, Mr Armstrong. Heard you had a little trouble down the way,' he said, frowning and waving his jailer from the chair behind his desk. Buck laughed as the rotund man hurried out of the lawman's way. Without stopping, but glaring at Buck, he scurried out the door.

'John giving you trouble again?' Brickey asked,

settling himself down and putting his heels up on the corner of the desk.

'Not really. He just took too much pleasure in warning me that Crown's foreman, or whatever he is, was likely going to be gunning for me. That doesn't make sense, but your jailer sure seems to think it does. Anyway, how'd you hear about what happened?'

'Eli Montague came into town last night late. Seems men from the Crown ranch caused some damage to his crops yesterday afternoon. He was telling me about you getting shot in the back. It doesn't look like it held you up too much.'

'No, I was damn lucky. All I got was a glancing blow. And then I had some good doctoring on top of that. I'm still a little stiff and sore and afraid I'll tear out the stitches Mrs Montague put in, but I'll be OK in a couple days.'

'Any idea who tried to gun you down?'

'Nope. Could have been someone from the Crown ranch; Ludel didn't seem to like me riding in to ask him about Lewis Clement. Somehow it just doesn't seem likely he and I will ever get to be good friends.'

Brickey laughed. 'Well, from what I hear, he'll have to stand in line to get his chance at you.' When Buck frowned, he chuckled. 'Seems our very own self-important banker, Kingston, doesn't think much of you, either.'

'Well, I can understand that. He wasn't happy when I threatened to boot his butt out of the newspaper office.'

'Yeah, Louise told me about that. Probably a good

thing you showed up when you did.'

'Oh, I doubt anything would have happened. Bullies rarely pick on anyone who's ready to call their bluff and I think that's one lady who won't be pushed.'

Brickey nodded, letting a little smile curve his lips. 'So you think it could be someone from Crown that shot you?'

'Well, no, it could also have been one of the farmers. I had a run in earlier in the day with young Balsom. He thought I was part of the trouble the farmers have been getting from the cattlemen. From what I heard later, he was mad enough and had gone riding out loaded for bear at about the right time. I hate to say it, but it could have been him. But it's true, I didn't do too well out at Crown's headquarters. I just don't know. But what's the trouble Montague had with Crown? That must have been after I left his place.'

'Yeah, he said it was along about dusk last night. He wanted me to go riding out to tell Ludel to stop causing the farmers trouble.' Brickey sighed 'But there isn't anything I can do. Hell, I'm only the sheriff here in town 'cause the town folk hired me; outside of the business area, I don't have a right to go acting like the law.'

Buck had run into this kind of problem before. Law came slower to small outlying farms and ranches than to the more organized towns. All too often those living outside the town limits had to rely on themselves for protection. The bigger the spread, the more men a rancher could call on for support and the stronger was his ability to make his own law.

'Some of these old men who came into the country when it was still wild and woolly,' Sheriff Brickey said dejectedly, 'don't understand that they can't just ride roughshod over people. I'd like to help Eli and his farmer friends, but there isn't anything I can do.'

Buck nodded slowly in agreement. 'What exactly happened?'

'Apparently a few Crown men tore out quite a stretch of fencing and ran a small herd of cattle into Montague's cornfield. Stick around a few minutes and I expect you'll be hearing all about it. I saw old man Balsom's wagon coming into town just a bit ago and I figure he'll be coming to see me about the same thing. The Balsoms and the Montagues' places lie almost side by side where the fence was cut.'

Buck frowned. He didn't like the idea of someone bothering the farmers, especially the family that had probably saved his life.

'Want a cup of coffee?' Brickey asked, and at Buck's nod got up. Handing the seated man a steaming mug, he had just sat back down when the office door crashed open.

'Sheriff, you just gotta do something,' Luke Balsom demanded, before noticing Buck sitting quietly to one side. 'Oh, didn't see you there, Armstrong. Heard you was back shot. Doesn't look like it did much damage.' Turning his attention back toward the lawman he let his words build up steam. 'Had a talk this morning with Eli and he says you don't think there's anything you can do. Well, I'm here to tell you, you'd better give it some more thought or you're gonna have a war on your hands.'

'Mr Balsom.' Sheriff Brickey waved him toward another chair. 'I'll tell you the same thing I told Eli Montague . . . there is nothing I can do about what happens outside of town. I'm the town's sheriff, not the territory's representative.'

Balsom heard the words and his posture lost its stiffness. Taking off his hat, he settled in the offered chair and sounding like all the air had gone out of him almost moaned. 'We gotta do something, Sheriff. If you can't help us, I just don't know what'll happen.'

For a minute nobody spoke, and then Buck asked, 'Are you certain it's men from the Crown ranch that's causing your people trouble?'

'Yeah. It started when that rancher Ludel came around and offered to buy us out. I heard later he made the same offer to Montague. Wanted to pay us a few hundred dollars, said we could move on and start over. His money would buy us new seed or shovels, he said. He didn't seem to think it was important that he was wanting our homes, places we'd all worked hard to build up. When we turned him down, he stopped buying our hay. We've heard he even got Garvey and some of the other ranchers to start cutting their own winter feed like they did before we came in. He told them we had some loco weed mixed in our hay. That was a lie. We've never sold anything but good hay. But we had to do something, so we loaded up our wagons and drove down to Durango to sell our crops. Took the best part of a week of travelling to make the deliveries and get back, but it paid enough to get us through the winter. It's been like that for better'n a year now. We was just getting by, until last evening. Now Eli's lost most of his corn crop and those steers got into my winter hay. Don't know how we'll survive now.' Balsom's head was down and Buck thought he had the look of a beaten man.

'Mr Balsom, I'm sorry,' Brickey said, his words coming slow. 'But there's nothing I can do.'

Buck sat for a bit. 'What did those Crown riders do? Run the herd through the fences they cut?'

'It ain't only that. Stampeding cattle into our fields was bad enough, but shooting up our houses, yelling and cursing, calling us names, scaring our women.' Balsom glanced up at Buck. 'I had to physically stop Royal from taking his rifle and going out to fight them. Can't blame the boy, but I couldn't let him go out to get killed, could I?'

'No. I hear you and Eli Montague have only been in the basin a few years. Do any of you own the land you're on?'

Balsom shook his head, again keeping his eyes on the floor. 'Naw. We're all homesteading. You know, take a hundred and sixty acres and make improvements and after five years the land is ours. We chose that land because nobody else wanted it. It's as dry as a bone but with the ditches we dug, we got all the water we need coming from the river. You can grow anything there now.'

'You got to hand it to them, Buck,' Sheriff Brickey confirmed, 'your farms are, what, Luke, quarter mile from the river?' Turning back to Buck he went on,

'They hand dug that big ditch and then a system of smaller ditches off that. It didn't take long and they had their first crop in.'

'And we've been there just a bit more'n three years.' Once again, looking up at Buck, his words became animated. 'And we was both doing pretty good, too. Selling our crops here in town or to the ranchers. We get together to help each other when it's needed, building barns, clearing the scrub or building the irrigation ditches. Until Ludel turned against us.'

'Has he ever said what's behind his trying to push you off your land?'

'Well, not really. He never has said what he wants. He was here before us and could have staked that flat land out, but he didn't. Like the sheriff says, it's a mite away from the river and I'd say he overlooked it because without water it wouldn't even support cheatgrass. Nearly all the land he'd claimed is either closer to the river or watered by springs and a few creeks. What he's got is good grazing. Our irrigation canals make the difference for our farms.'

Sheriff Brickey placed both hands flat on his desk. 'Well, Mr Balsom, I'll tell you the same thing I told Montague: telegraph the territorial governor's office. Any help will have to come from there, I'm afraid.'

Balsom slowly stood up and stood for a moment turning his hat in his hands. 'That homestead idea sounded pretty good. You pay your eighteen dollars and are given a quarter section. All it is, though, is the government betting the land they say they own against our eigthteen dollars that our families and us will starve to death before we make it the five years. Just like a government, full of empty promises, take your money and then don't offer any protection.' Nodding at the sheriff and Buck, he shuffled out the door.

'Damn it all to hell,' Brickey grimaced, slapping his hand flat on the desk top in frustration. 'Those folks deserve better than that.' Looking out through the dirty window he watched the rumbling ore wagons go by. 'Wonder what caused Ludel to go after them now like he did.'

'Yeah, I was thinking the same thing. I wonder if maybe my going out and asking about Lewis Clement had anything to do with it. If it was someone from the Crown ranch who shot me out of the saddle, he might have wanted to punish the Montagues for patching me up.' Standing up slowly, he frowned. 'I think I'll give my back a couple of days' rest and then go out and see what I can do.'

'Don't go getting deeper in trouble with those Crown riders. If your back-shooter did come from there, it won't do you any good to become a target again.'

Buck carefully settled his Stetson in place and smiled. 'According to your chubby jailer, I've still got trouble coming my way from the other direction. He tells me that Crown's man, Reynaldo, is coming gunning for me in a couple days.' Chuckling a bit he pushed open the office door. 'Seems like if I don't get it from one end, I'm sure to from the other.'

CHAPTER 10

The following two days were quiet ones for Buck, days he let his back heal. Both mornings he enjoyed breakfast at Mrs Ritter's and then strolled down the street to the Silverton Hotel, settling comfortably in one of the rocking chairs on the porch. Except for coffee with Sheriff Brickey and once passing the time of day with Louise Clement over at the newspaper office, he simply sat and watched the town.

This morning, just sitting wasn't enough. Having the stitches out of his back, he felt like it was time to be earning his keep. He wanted to do something for the Montague and Balsom families and Louise Clement was still counting on him finding out something about her brother.

Earlier that morning, after filling himself on a breakfast of ham, eggs, a stack of sourdough pancakes and two cups of coffee, Buck asked directions to the town doctor.

'Now I'm not sure that's a good thing,' Mrs Ritter warned him when he asked. 'You don't look like there's much wrong with you but that might not be true you go letting that old fool lay a hand on you. He's the one who worked over my Andrew, you know,' and with lips pursed, nodded her head strongly. 'Andrew never missed a day's work in his life. Healthy as a horse until he went to see that man who calls himself a doctor. Bah, he's a doctor then I'm Florence Nightingale. No, sir. Not a day sick in his life.'

Buck had to ask. 'What ailed your husband that he went to the doctor?'

'I don't know. One day he woke up groaning and moaning. Said he had an ache in his stomach. Stayed home from work and I gave him a physic, the same kind my momma used to give us kids when we had a stomach ache from eating too many green apples. It didn't do any good, though. He didn't get much sleep that night and the next morning he was hurting worse. So he went to see old Doc Wilcox.'

'Is that the only doctor in town?'

'Yes, Doctor Wilcox, he calls himself. Treat any living being, whether man or beast. He couldn't help my Andrew, though. Gave him a bottle of foul-smelling stuff and sent him home. After another night and morning of hurting and drinking that so-called medicine, Andrew died the next day. In the late afternoon it was. I threw the bottle out after Andrew was buried.'

'I thought someone told me your husband was killed in a mining accident.'

'Nope. He died right here in this house. I heard the mining accident story, too and I think it was handed out just so people wouldn't blame Dr Wilcox.

What's wrong with you, anyway?' she asked, slipping the question in without taking a breath.

'Mrs Montague stitched up a wound on my back and I think it'll heal better if that thread was taken out.'

'Well, I don't know nothing about doctoring, but I do know about sewing and such. As I recall, that Mrs Montague sews a fine stitch. Her work is among the first that sells at the church bazaars. Here, take off that shirt and let me take a look. That is if you're not too shy to be half dressed in the parlour of an old widow woman.'

Buck chuckled and started unbuttoning his shirt.

'Yes,' the woman murmured softly while looking at his back, 'those stitches are the work of a real seamstress. She used black silk so they show up real good. Let me get my sewing scissors,' Mrs Ritter said, going to a dark wooden cabinet.

'Now that's an interesting wound,' she muttered, as she went to work. Buck could hear the snip-snip as she cut the thread and felt a slight tug as each of the pieces was pulled free.

'It's certainly scabbed over nicely, but you'll have a bit of a scar when it's all healed up.' With a final pull the last of the stitches was removed and she told Buck he could put his shirt back on. 'Now that's a lot better than letting that horse doctor get his hands on you.'

'I thank you,' Buck said, tucking his shirttails in and settling his gunbelt comfortably around his waist. He was about to say something else when the front door swung open and Sheriff Brickey came in.

'Well, good morning, Sheriff,' Mrs Ritter greeted him, 'you were almost in time to catch this fine young man half undressed in my front parlour.'

Buck's chuckle died when he caught the serious look on the lawman's face. 'There a problem, Sheriff?'

'Yeah. Ludel and his crew just rode into town. I had a talk with John about what he told you, but when I saw that Reynaldo strutting across to the Gold Dust Saloon, I thought I'd better let you know.'

'I appreciate that, Sheriff. But it's too early for me to be visiting any saloon. I've just had some expert medical attention and was thinking about heading toward the hotel porch for some recuperation.' Thanking the landlady again and settling his hat at an acceptable angle, the two men left the boarding-house, Buck explaining about getting the stitches taken out while they walked.

'Well, Sheriff, I was really on my way to the restaurant for a cup of coffee, but didn't want to hurt Mrs Ritter's feelings. You have time to join me for a cup?'

'No. I think I'd better get back to the office. I'm trying to write a letter to the territorial governor about the trouble brewing with old man Ludel and that group of farmers. Don't know it'll do any good, but something's going to have to be done before it gets any worse.'

'Yeah, I've been giving that some thought myself. Those folks were real quick to help me and, well, I'd like to help them. Just can't think of what to do, though.'

'Don't be forgetting, it might have been the son of

one of those farmers who took that shot at you.'

'No, I haven't forgotten that. It doesn't seem likely and it certainly wasn't someone from the Montague place. I guess a letter is about all that can be done.'

The two men walked down the street together until Brickey left Buck at his office door. Buck stopped for a moment to wait for a rumbling ore wagon pass by. Thinking about the noise of the ore wagons pulled by six horse teams, churning up the surface of Main Street, he shook his head in disgust. Almost as if on a tight schedule, the wagons went by, wide iron rims of the wheels cutting deeply in the thick mud coming in from the north and, after dumping their load at the stamp mill outside of town to the south, barely leaving a mark on the return trip. The rattle of chains and yelling of the teamsters made it difficult to hear the regular beat of the huge stamping heads as they crushed the ore into powder.

It certainly wasn't, he thought with repugnance, like the quiet of one of his fishing streams up in the high country. Well then, he said silently, let's get this over with and get back up there.

While he was standing watching the wagons go by, what he didn't know was that others were watching him.

Brass Kingston stood looking out the window of his office right above the door to his bank with his back to the room, ignoring the man who filled the chair across from the banker's desk.

'Dammit, Dutch, how could you miss?'

'Dunno, boss. Had him centred, just sitting there daydreaming it looked like. Just when I touched the trigger something made him move. I knocked him flying, but it must've not got him straight.'

'I knew sooner or later someone would be coming up here from the capitol. It has to be him. He's telling everyone he's here to look for Lewis Clement, but I figure he's the governor's man. I know for a fact that after the second hold-up, Baker wrote the governor's office demanding help. If there's one thing Governor Sturgis likes it's money and the gold that comes out of here; he makes sure he gets his share, I reckon.'

'Yeah, but there ain't nothing he can find, is there?'

Without turning around, Kingston shook his head.

Dutch Voles didn't like it when the banker disregarded him like that, wouldn't even turn around, just stood there staring out the window. Dammit, he may be a banker now but it wasn't so many years ago that it was Kingston leading the gang. Now he was a big shot banker and what was left of the bunch following him was Dutch Voles. Well, maybe it was time to shake the big man up a little.

'Kingston, there could be trouble coming from another direction. The boys aren't too happy the way things are going. When you brought us over, you promised a lot more'n what we've got so far. And you never said anything about someone coming up from the capitol. Next thing you know, there'll be a slew of soldiers coming in to move the gold bullion. The boys don't like the way things're going.'

'Now, Dutch, you just relax a bit. The way I've got it planned, the first two times was just to prime the pump, you might say. Now Baker and the mine owners are afraid to ship. They're holding back. Just as I planned. They'll hold back until they are convinced they can get a shipment through. That'll be the big haul and the one we're waiting for. We can all retire with our shares of that. All you and the boys have to do is wait and let me do my work.'

Getting out of the chair, the outlaw leader settled his gunbelt and then stood with his hands resting on the butts of his six-guns.

'Well, they don't like it. It's hard to make them understand how the gold from those two raids is sitting here in your bank and they can't even come into town for a drink of rotgut.' Holding up a hand to ward off Kingston's response, he went on, 'I know, I know. That's the way it has to be and that's what we agreed on. But it isn't setting easy with them. Just want you to know. That's all.'

'OK, so now I know. So now you go back out there and tell them to be patient. When I can work out how to make Baker feel safe, they'll have to be ready. I'll get word to you the regular way and then everyone'll be happy.'

'How're you planning on doing that? Making the mine owners think the time is right to ship?'

Kingston was back at the window, looking down as the tall cowboy crossed the street and went into the hotel restaurant. 'Oh, I think that'll work itself out,' he said softly. 'And more'n likely in the next week or so, too. It's that big cowboy that has me a mite worried. We can't very well take another shot at him. People'd begin to wonder. Old fat John over at the jail has been talking about that Mexican who works for Ludel having his own reason to want to see the end of him. Maybe when Crown comes into town today he'll do the job for us.'

Turning to look over his shoulder the banker nodded toward his office door. 'But you'd better get back to camp, Dutch. And don't be coming back into town again, you hear? It's too dangerous. If someone were to see you it'd spoil everything.'

'Yeah, but if we don't get something going pretty soon, the men'll be wanting to take matters into their own hands. And that'll spoil things for sure.'

'I'm counting on you to keep them under control, Dutch. I'll get word to you when the next shipment is being sent.'

Kingston's voice hardened. 'And as far as your men are concerned,' he added, 'remind them of what happened to the bunch that was attacking the shipments coming out of Ophir. I've been busy keeping the businessmen from thinking too much about forming a vigilante group, but it's getting harder. Some of them are losing business because of the first two hold-ups. If a few strangers show up, hanging around town, I don't know if I could stop them from thinking about taking matters into their own hands.'

Voles cuffed his worn dirty grey Stetson and grimaced. 'You made your point. We lost a lot of good men to those blasted vigilantes over in Ophir. I'll keep the boys out at camp, but you had better make something work soon. They know the gold from the two raids is sitting in your bank and more than one has held up a bank before.'

Without waiting for a response, the outlaw pushed through the door and disappeared down the back stairs.

'Damn,' Kingston muttered, turning back to the window. 'Damn fools.' Standing with his hands clasped behind his back, he watched the street below and thought about the future. Once he had the gold from the next raid, he'd have enough. With the men from town formed into a strong vigilante party at his back, Dutch Voles and his gang of ruffians wouldn't be able to get near him. All he had to do is think of a way to get that big galoot down there to do what he wanted him to do.

Even after the big breakfast, a piece of fresh baked apple pie was too good to pass up. Buck was just finishing the last crumb when Nell Ludel pulled out a chair across the table from him and sat down.

'I'm so glad to find you here,' she said, her voice soft and throaty. 'You saved my life and I didn't even get a chance to thank you. Mr Ludel is, well, he is very abrupt sometimes.'

'Yeah, I noticed.' Buck frowned and sat back in his chair. Most of the stiffness he'd felt in the back of his shoulder seemed to have gone along with the stitches. Slowly he moved his upper left arm around a little, testing if there was any tightness around the scab. Other than a twinge when the skin pulled with the movement, it felt almost normal.

'You have to understand,' Mrs Ludel went on, after ordering a cup of tea, 'he is, well, he's not a young man and he doesn't like it when I get friendly with any other man. It's normal, I suppose, but he just won't believe me when I tell him I'm happy being his wife.'

Buck wanted to ask why she was out there with men like Big Carl and Hugo, but decided it wasn't any of his business. This young woman would be too much for any old man to trust too far no matter how big his ranch was. He didn't say anything, just sipped the last of his coffee.

'Oh, I know, it didn't look good, my being with those two hired hands. But you see, sometimes I feel I'm being held captive at Crown. This is the first time Mr Ludel has brought me into town in three months. I'm used to being around people and being able to go shopping and, well, I miss St Louis.'

Buck carefully placed his empty cup on the table and started to stand up.

'Please' – the woman put her hand on his, holding him – 'I need help and there's no one I can turn to.'

'Ma'am.' Buck sat back and slowly shook his head. 'One of the quickest ways of getting shot is for a man to get between another man and his lawfully wedded wife. If you've got a problem with your husband, then you've got to figure a way out of it. But don't go look-ing to me to help you. Now,' he said brusquely as he stood, 'it's been nice meeting you but I'll be on my way.'

Paying for his pie and coffee, he was taking his Stetson from the hat tree by the front door when the door slammed open and Rufus Ludel came storming in. The tall Mexican, Reynaldo, followed right behind.

The rancher saw only his wife sitting, holding a thin china teacup to her lips. Reynaldo stopped a few steps into the room and turned to face Buck. A thin smile slowly lifted his lips.

'Ah, *señor*, we meet again, no?' At his words, Ludel stopped and spun around.

'You,' he snarled. Buck wondered if the rancher had ever in his life smiled. 'What the blazes are you doing here?'

'Why, I suppose the same as you, having a cup of coffee,' he said innocently.

Reynaldo chuckled softly. Buck noticed the man's right thumb was hooked over his belt buckle, his hand inches from his holstered gun butt.

Ludel let his eyes study Buck and then looked down at the table, using a finger to push at the empty coffee cup with a finger. 'You been talking with my wife?'

'We did touch briefly on the last time we met. Seems she felt some gratitude for my having come along right when I did.'

Looking down at his wife, the rancher made a quick motion with his hand. 'Get your things, we're through here.'

'But Mr Ludel, I haven't finished my tea.'

'Don't matter. I shouldn't have brought you to town. Seems I can't trust you not to go meeting up with one drifter or another no matter where you are. Get going, we're heading back to the ranch.'

Slowly, taking her time, Mrs Ludel stood up still holding the teacup. Keeping her eyes directly on her husband, she sipped the last of the drink before replacing the cup on its saucer. Buck couldn't help but smile when he heard Reynaldo's harsh chuckle.

'Reynaldo,' Ludel's voice carried across the room, 'shoot him.'

Buck laughed out loud as he reached up to thumb the thong from his Colt's hammer. 'I'll say this for you, Mr Ludel, you're a man who likes to make quick decisions. First time it was "hang him" and now its "shoot him" . . . almost enough to make me think you don't like me.'

Reynaldo turned his body so he was squarely facing Buck. 'You are a brave *hombre, señor.* Señor Ludel doesn't like men to speak with his wife. You may die with that thought on your mind.'

Buck let his smile grow as he slowly shook his head. 'I doubt it,' he said quietly. 'Tell me, Reynaldo, from the saddle you sit and the way you follow along, I'd say you're more this man's bodyguard than a ranch foreman. That true? If he tells you to shoot me, you'll do it?'

'*Sí, señor.* Mr Ludel tells me something, I do it.'

'And for this you get paid a pretty good wage, I'll bet.'

Reynaldo smiled and nodded, not taking his eyes off Buck's.

'Tell me,' Buck went on, 'does the owner of Crown owe you any money? Say last month's salary?' The Mexican gunman frowned but didn't respond.

'Reason I ask is to give you something to think about. You see, it's almost a certainty that if you pull on me, you likely won't collect those wages. Or get paid for shooting me, either.'

'Don't stand there jawing,' Ludel snarled, 'shoot him.'

Reynaldo stood still, watching Buck, waiting.

'You see,' Buck said, ignoring Ludel and watching the gunman's eyes, 'if you were to move your hand, even just a little bit, I'd have to shoot your boss. Now, it's pretty clear you'd get a slug in me but there're a couple things to think about. First, your boss would be as dead as I could make him, so no more easy paydays, and second, I'm a very determined man.' Buck let his voice harden. 'And a determined man, even with a bullet in him will still be dangerous. I'd get at least one shot in you and at this range, well, we'd both be dead. Think about it.'

'Think about it, hell!' Ludel shouted. 'Shoot him!'

For a long moment Reynaldo simply stood and stared at Buck. Then slowly he let his hand drop to his side and straightened up, a smile fluttering across his face.

'Damn you, Reynaldo,' Ludel was sputtering. He didn't like being ignored. 'You're getting too high and mighty. Don't forget who you work for.'

'No, Señor Ludel, it is you I am thinking of. I believe this *hombre* would do as he says and he is right, I haven't been paid yet.'

Nell Ludel standing across the table from her husband chuckled behind her hand. The sound brought the rancher's head around. 'Reynaldo,' he said softly, keeping his eyes on her and with all anger gone from his voice, 'get the buggy. Mrs Ludel and I will be returning to the ranch. You can stay and bring the supplies.'

Reynaldo nodded to Buck as he stepped aside a little to let Reynaldo pass.

'Ah, *señor*,' the smiling Mexican said softly, 'you are truly a man. Today I will not shoot you, but there is always *mañana*, no?'

CHAPTER 11

Again relaxing on the hotel porch, Buck watched the town fill up with families from outlying ranches and farms coming to do their weekly shopping and visiting. Many would stay overnight, sleeping in their wagons, or camping just outside of town, and attend church the next morning. Saturday was the day for women to meet and exchange gossip and men to share a drink at the Gold Dust Saloon. With the Saturday night dance, it was also a time for courting.

Buck had seen the Montague family ride in, followed a short time later by the Balsoms. When Eli Montague and Luke Balsom left their wives at the general store and headed for the saloon, he got up and followed.

'Well, it looks like you're a fast healer,' Montague greeted Buck, as the three men found places at the long mahogany bar and ordered their drinks.

'It can all be blamed on the excellent care given by the women of your family. All I had to do is sit around and let things happen.'

Balsom watched Buck carefully. 'Have you figured

out who shot you?' he asked quietly.

'I don't have any idea, but your son Royal sure has a good friend in Miss Montague. I was hardly awake and aware and she was working hard to convince me Royal couldn't be the shooter.' Seeing that his words didn't change the other man's frown, Buck smiled. 'But somehow I never did think it was your boy. Anyone who'd want to prove his point face to face with fists would not be the kind who would later back shoot anyone. No, there's something else going on that I don't know about.'

Balsom relaxed a little. 'Thank you for that,' he said, letting a small smile lift his lips a bit. 'Royal is a good boy. Well, a young man, really. He just hasn't learned yet not to jump to conclusions.'

'Anyway,' Buck said, after sipping his beer and wiping the foam from his upper lip, 'I wanted to talk with you two a little about the troubles you've been having with Crown. It isn't any of my business, but your wife and daughter didn't have to take me in and sew me up. Do you have any idea what Ludel has on his mind?'

Eli Montague frowned before answering. 'Not really. Luke Balsom and I figure he wants our land, now that we've put water on it. He's just greedy and wants to put his cattle on our land. It could be more than that, too. There's that talk of a rail line being brought in. Crown land is a little higher than where we are and any spur line would have to cross over near the bluffs that our farms back up to. That would mean Crown would still have to drive their cattle south of us to a railhead. If he could get rid of us and take our land, he'd have the railhead on his property. He could be thinking about that.'

'This last attack you were telling Sheriff Brickey about, is that the kind of thing that's been going on?'

Balsom shook his head. 'No, that was the worst yet. Cutting the fences and letting a few of his cattle into the fields is what we've had to put up with until now. No telling what Ludel is planning to do next.'

'Well, that's what I wanted to talk to you about. I don't have much to do right now, there hasn't been anything I can do about finding Lewis Clement, so I thought I might see what can be done about your problem with Crown.'

'That would put you in some kind of danger, wouldn't it? That little bit of doctoring my wife and daughter did was just what we'd do for anyone who needed it. What's the real reason you'd want to take on our problem?' Montague asked. 'What's in it for you?'

'Mr Montague, that little bit of doctoring, as you call it, may have saved my life. That might not count much for you, but it certainly does for me. Other than that, I want nothing.' Holding both hands out, palms up, he smiled. 'Just look at it like payment for bringing me in and fixing up my back.'

'Well, I don't know.' Balsom was showing himself to be overly cautious. 'I think the best thing would be to wait. Sheriff Brickey said he'd write to the governor.' Shaking his head, he frowned into his beer. 'I thank you for your offer, but I think that'd be the best thing for us to do.'

Buck looked from one man to the other. Neither

met his eyes. 'OK, if that's what you think is best. It's your farms. Here, let me buy you another glass of beer.'

Supper that night at the boarding-house was beef steak, cooked just the way Buck liked it, well done on the outside and bloody when he cut into the middle. Sitting in one of the chairs on the porch after the meal, Buck slowly rolled a cigarette and thought about the day. Quiet settled over the town as the last empty wagon passed by, heading back toward the mines. Dusk, with enough sunlight still hiding the stars, was a good time of day, he thought, to sit and think.

He knew he'd been lucky in his little set-to with the Crown owner, Ludel. That Mexican gunman, Reynaldo, wasn't someone to fool with. A wrong move by anyone and there would have been a shooting. It was clear that the middle-aged rancher had a real problem with his young wife. Jealous of her every move, Buck thought, didn't allow him much time to be comfortable. It was clear that the tighter he held on, the more damage that was being done to their marriage.

But what did he know about marriage? Smiling to himself, he thought about the few times he'd come close to getting into double harness. Nope, he thought, not while there was some good fishing to be had.

It didn't look like there'd be much fishing in a while, though. Finding out what happened to Lewis Clement just wasn't working out. Louise Clement would likely end up marrying the sheriff, but not knowing about her brother would probably always be riding her. Ah, he sighed quietly, young love. Louise and Cord Brickey, Elizabeth Montague and, what was her beau's name? Charlie Baker. Flicking his cigarette butt out into the street he smiled. They're all more than likely out at the dance, enjoying themselves. Too bad old man Ludel couldn't see his way clear to bring his wife in for the affair.

Thinking about that, Buck frowned. Ludel was a very angry man. Afraid he was going to lose something and holding on as tight as he was, it was likely he would lose out, sooner or later.

'Mr Armstrong?' someone called from the street. Full darkness had come unseen and Buck, caught unaware, could just barely make out the shadowed bulk of a man standing next to the front gate. Sitting where he was in the shadows of the porch, out of the light streaming softly through a boarding-house widow, Buck knew he would be hard to see. Slipping the thong from his holstered six-gun, he leaned to one side a little so if he had to pull iron, he would have room.

Softly, watching the outline of the man standing on the other side of the fence, he softly answered. 'Yeah, I'm here.'

'I'm Charlie Baker. We haven't met, but I'd like to talk to you, if you don't mind.'

'Sure, come on up on to the porch.'

'Well, that's the thing, you see. I would prefer to keep our conversation quiet. Would you mind meeting me down at the stamp mill in a while? Say half an hour or so? I'd like to talk to you, but it'd be best if nobody saw us together.'

Buck sat for a moment, thinking about getting shot in the back. He'd not met Baker and had no reason to think the man had any cause to be a danger. Maybe he knew something about Lewis Clement's vanishing. 'Yeah, I guess I could do that.'

'Good. There's a barn around behind the main office. Come around back and knock on the door. They'll be closed, but we'll be waiting.'

Before Buck could ask who the "we" would be, Baker turned and walked away. Settling back in the chair, thinking about the request for a secret meeting, he decided he'd be very careful about walking into any strange barn. Especially when he didn't know what he'd be walking into. Maybe, he thought coming to his feet, it wouldn't hurt to get there a little early.

CHAPTER 12

Except for the lanterns lighting up the interiors of a couple of the town's larger saloons, all the windows along the main street were dark. Buck took his time walking down the boardwalk, not making any more noise than was necessary. He hadn't been anywhere near the stamp mill, but knew it had to be a short distance beyond the southern end of the business section. Stepping off the end of the plank walk, he could see the tall mill building off to his left. Off to one side the other way, the double doors of a large building were open and light streamed out. He could hear the yells of people having fun backed up by music. Apparently Baker hadn't gone to the dance.

The thick crescent of the moon had come up from behind the mountains and in the weak light given off by the orb he could clearly see how the deep-ruts of the wagon road pointed the way to the mill. Staying to one side, out of the dust of the road, he made his way toward the darkness of the cluster of buildings. Getting closer, he thought he could see a soft glow coming from one low shed that was separated from the larger structures. Angling in that direction, with the thong off the hammer of his Colt, he saw that the faint light was coming through a window. Keeping in the dark, he made his way to the shed and peeked into window. A lantern, turned down so the flame was nearly out, sat on a desk that was covered with paper and record books. This, he figured, had to be the mill's office.

Careful not to trip over anything, he walked around the shed. The faint noise coming from the dance far behind him somehow made the silence around the dark angular buildings feel deep and thick. Stopping to let his eyes adjust to the blackness, he waited. Not focusing on what was directly ahead of him, he soon began to seee the barn out of the corner of his eye, its wide, tall doors closed. Leaning back against the rough plank wall of the office shed, he waited and watched.

For what seemed like a long time he put off moving. Finally deciding the half-hour had passed, he pushed away from the shed and walked back toward the double doors. The outline of a small door to the far side had to be the one Baker had wanted him to knock on. Standing to one side, he reached out his left hand and rapped his knuckles against the rough wood. The door swung open almost at once.

'Armstrong? Come on in,' the faint light of a shrouded lantern gave off enough light so Buck could see the man motioning him in.

With the door closed, another man lifted the sacking from a lantern. The first man Buck saw was

Sheriff Brickey, who was leaning against the side of a buckboard. Two other men stood next to the lawman. Buck didn't recognize one of them, but the other was the banker, Brass Kingston. The man Buck took to be Baker stood facing him with his hands on his hips.

'I apologize for all the secrecy, Mr Armstrong,' Baker said, stepping forward and holding out his hand. 'I'm Charlie Baker. Thank you for coming down like this.'

'I imagine,' Brickey said, half smiling to soften his words, 'that after getting shot in the back you took your time and scouted out the place pretty carefully. Am I right?'

'Well, I did look it over a bit,' Buck said, glancing at the sheriff. Glancing at Kingston, he nodded and then looked back at Baker. 'What's this all about, anyway?'

'We've decided to send another shipment out to Durango. Tonight with the dance going on and most everyone over there having fun, we thought this might be a good time. I head up the mine-owners' association,' he went on, pointing to the others one at a time, 'and the others are Burton Alvord, owner of the Glory Jane Mine, Brass Kingston of the Silverton Bank and Howard Rankeillor, who owns the Bonanza Mine. You know Sheriff Brickey, I believe.'

'Yes,' Kingston cut in, his voice harsh, 'Armstrong and I have met. And I have to say again, I don't see what he has to do with this shipment. He doesn't have any interest in our gold and letting a stranger in on what was supposed to be a secret shipment, well, I just hope you know what you're doing.'

The man identified as Rankeillor chuckled. 'Yah, Mr Kingston. I like that . . . "our gold". The gold we have in those strong boxes is gold from the Glory Jane and the Bonanza. Charlie Baker, the son of my good friend, milled it. It has never gone through your bank, so I wonder how it became "our gold"?'

'Gentlemen,' Baker held up his hands, 'let's not get into that. The four of us make up the committee and it's our job to get the bullion to the bank in Durango. We've been through all this before. Mr Kingston is here because he is representing the Durango Bank. I'm sure when he said "our gold" he was speaking in the broadest of terms.'

Buck heard Brickey's soft chuckle.

'I can't say I find this at all interesting,' the cowboy said, shaking his head slowly side to side, 'but the question is still out there, what am I doing here?'

'Mr Armstrong, the last two shipments were lost to a gang of hold-up men. We think they were the same men both times. Now, we had kept secret when those shipments were to go. Nobody outside of this committee was to know. But someone did and we lost both and ended up with too many of our hired guards being killed. We've held off sending any more gold down the trail but we're getting too great an amount to keep putting off making a shipment any longer. We've got bills to pay, payrolls to meet. This morning we decided to make it different this time.'

'You decided,' Kingston insisted. 'I was not consulted and, if I had been, I'd have talked against it. I still don't see how bringing in someone none of us know is going to make the shipment any more secure.'

'That's the point, Brass,' Burton Alvord explained. 'Mr Armstrong is new in town. Sheriff Brickey stands by him and tells us he is a good man. That's enough for me. Being new, nobody would expect him to be involved with any gold shipment. We, the three of us, talked it over and all agreed on it. So, enough with the arguing. Let's get this going before we find ourselves sending out the wagons in the morning light.'

'Just as long as you all know that I don't like bringing this man in and don't know why you want to trust him. I don't like this man Armstrong, and I don't want anything to do with it. I'm going home.' Kingston, his face flushed with anger, stomped out slamming the barn down shut behind him.

'Ah, this man is just not open to anything unless it is something he thought of first,' Alvord shook his head. 'But he's right. There is no reason for all of us to be here. Charlie, we leave it all in your hands. Mr Armstrong, the only thing we want is to get our gold to Durango. We hope this can be done without anyone getting shot, unless it is the hold-up men who are killed. That would be good.' The other mine owner, Rankeillor, nodded his agreement and the two men left the barn.

'Well, Charlie,' the sheriff said, still leaning back with his arms crossed in front of him, 'apparently it's all your show. What now?'

'The plan is simple, I've got two wagons, the one

you're leaning against and the other over there. The bullion has been packed in those boxes,' he explained, pointing to four wooden boxes. Heavy looking padlocks secured the steel bands that wrapped each box.

'Two of those boxes contain rocks,' he continued. 'We'll load the gold in one wagon and the fake boxes in the other. That way nobody will know which is the real shipment. The two wagons will go by different routes, one down the wagon road and the other over the old stage route.'

'And the three of us will be guarding both these wagons?'

'No, Sheriff, having you along wouldn't help. The hold-up men would spot you and know which one to hit. No, I have a dozen men waiting over in the cook shack. Six will ride with one and six with the other. We're paying them an extra bonus for making the trip. Buck, we're willing to pay you fifty dollars for taking one of the wagons.'

'Then you don't need me any more?' Sheriff Brickey asked.

'No. But thank you for helping me guard the gold while it was here. It'll be best, I think, if only Buck and I know which wagon has the shipment.'

Brickey stood up and started for the door. 'Then I guess I'll go see if I can have a dance or two with a certain newspaper lady. Good night and good luck.'

Buck shook his head. 'I'm happy to help out, but somehow I don't know if letting you talk me into this is a good thing.'

'I know it's asking a lot, but I don't know what else

to do. We've got to get this gold out of here. The mines can't keep working without operating capital. You're the only person I could think of to ask.'

Buck stood thinking about it a moment and then nodded. 'Well, like your banker friend said, I don't like it much, but I'll help.'

The boxes were heavy and it took both men to lift each one into the two buckboards. Wiping the dust off his hands after the last box was secured, Buck looked at the stamp-mill owner. 'OK, do I take the real shipment' – he nodded toward the front buckboard – 'or the fake one?'

Baker frowned. 'You could tell? I tried to keep both boxes about the same.'

'It's hard to keep a box of rocks from rattling a little. Yeah, I could tell. You know, there's something that bothers me about this. Your committee thinks the outlaws knew when you were making the other shipments?'

'Well, we didn't make any secret of the first one. The two mines hadn't been producing much gold until a vein was hit in the Bonanza. Until then all that had been taken was free gold, in pockets. It wasn't long after that vein was found that the Glory Jane ran into it. The geology in both mines is about the same and all the ore is made up of quartz containing free gold and sulphuretes. The ore body as a whole forms a mass of clay slate crossed by quartz veins and seams of all sizes.' Baker explained, getting excited about it. 'Something like seventy per cent is free gold and the concentrates assay out to vary from twenty to sixty dollars per ton, chiefly in gold.'

'Now that sounds good,' Buck smiled, 'but some-how it doesn't interest me much. Guess I'd care a lot more if it were my gold we were discussing. No, what I'm thinking about is how to get your gold to the bank and keep me alive at the same time. From what I hear, it's clear there's someone in town telling the gang when the gold will be taken out. Tell me again, your committee decided this morning to make this shipment?'

'I hate to think it, but yes, there has to be someone I know and trust working with that gang of outlaws. That's why we want this trip to be done at night. And yes, Burton rode down from the Glory Jane with the first ore wagon this morning. He's worried that he won't be able to make the next payroll unless he ships his specie. We rode up to the Bonanza and met with Howard.'

'And the three of you came up with this idea. Send out two wagons and hope the outlaw gang picks the wrong one?'

'It's the only thing we could think of. There were eight men who hit us the first time and one was killed. The next time only seven men were counted, so we believe it's the same men. If they see two wagons going out, there isn't enough of them to stop both wagons.'

'When did you bring your banker friend into the plan?'

'Well, we had to tell him we were making a ship-ment. It's the bank's boxes that we ship in. He was angry that we cut him out, but we couldn't find him earlier. Why are you asking?'

'Kingston and I got off on the wrong foot and don't like each other much. I was just thinking, you've tried to keep this shipment a secret and right now only five of us know it's going out. And only the two of us know which wagon the gold is in. Wouldn't it be safer if only two people knew where the gold really was?'

'What do you mean?'

'Maybe it's my dislike for Kingston, but I don't trust him. He knows the shipment is going and that it's in one of these buckboards guarded by your men. OK, what if neither of the buckboards had the gold? If all four boxes carried rocks? If word got to the raiders and they stopped either of the wagons, simply moving the boxes a little and they'd know right away they didn't have the gold. Now if your guards didn't put up a fight and did as they were told, they should be safe.'

'Where would the gold be if not in the boxes? This shipment has to reach Durango.'

'You're using mules to pull the wagons?' Baker nodded. 'OK, I'm going to have to go back to the stable to get my horse. Let's say I bring a couple of extra horses, ones we can use as pack horses. You have anything we can put the gold in? What say we replace the gold with more rocks and send the wagons out. You tell your men not to put up a fight. Meanwhile, you and I take the pack animals by a route that a wagon couldn't go. There must be some old trail south.'

Baker stood for a moment looking at Buck, thinking. 'That means only you and I know where the gold is. One or the other of the wagons gets stopped, if that is, the outlaws learn of the shipment at all, but find nothing. That also means I've got to trust you a lot more than I'd planned on.'

Buck smiled, holding his hands out palms up. 'Yeah, that's right. But I'll be the first to tell you that I have no use for gold. You offered me fifty dollars to make the trip, that's enough. And if it'd make you feel any better, you can even ride behind me all the way.'

Nothing was said for a few minutes while the mill owner thought it over.

'Sheriff Brickey seems to think you can be trusted. I'll take a chance on you for two reasons: first, because the gold has to get to the bank in Durango, and second, because I'll be right behind you with a rifle ready to stop you.'

Buck chuckled and let his hands drop. 'OK, then let's get that gold out of those boxes and into some kind of saddle-bags.'

'There's only one thing, though,' Baker said, climbing into the back of the buckboard. 'I know how to get out of town without being seen, but that trail winds around the back side of a mountain range. It's a long ride all the way to Durango. Probably take us two full days of riding. And we can't sit around and wait until the general store opens to get enough food.'

Buck nodded and waited for Baker to finish his thought.

'The wagons take the best part of a day and a half to two days to get there,' the stamp-mill owner said

111

after a bit, 'That is if they take it easy on the horses and stop overnight. Of course, if they're hit early on, then they could turn around and come on back. There's no need for them to go on after the outlaws figure out they aren't carrying any gold.'

'And that means they wouldn't have any need for extra grub. Can you split off enough to feed us for the trip?'

'Yes, I can do that while you get the horses. But be quiet about it.'

'The stableman keeps a few of the horses he rents out back in a corral. I'll borrow a couple of those.'

Removing the gold bars from the boxes and filling the boxes with rocks took a while. Most of the time was spent trying to find enough heavy bags to put the gold into. Buck, keeping off the main street, returned with his black stud horse and two hack-amore-led horses by the time Charlie Baker had bags of food, two soogans and the bagged gold ready. While Buck was getting the horses, the guards had been given their orders and started on their way, each with two riders, rifles at the ready leading the way, and three others bringing up the rear. Charlie Baker made it clear they were not to put up a fight if the outlaws held them up.

Loading the pack horses was quickly accomplished and the small parade with Buck leading the way quietly left the dark, silent cluster of buildings.

The going was easy for the first half-hour or so. Buck followed the dim moonlit trail away from town, heading toward a distant low range of mountains. Coming to a wide, shallow creek, however, he stopped.

'Well, Charlie Baker, here's where the going gets tough. I don't have any notion which way to go. Somehow it looks like you're going to have to extend that bit of trust and take the lead. I suppose we could wait until morning and you could give out the directions, but that'll only make the ride a lot longer. What do you say?'

CHAPTER 13

Muttering curses under his breath and giving Buck a long sideways look as he rode past, Baker, with his back straight and stiff, took the lead. Buck chuckled and making sure the pack horses were following docilely along, fell in behind.

The moon, still a few days from being anywhere near full, gave off just enough light for the riders to see the trail. Most everything else was in dark shadow, though. The two men rode silently, keeping the horses at a steady ground-eating walk. For a time the trail climbed in a gradual set of switchbacks, finally topping out on a sharp backbone of a ridge that was bare of trees or brush. Stopping to give the horses a breather, Buck swung down and checked the loads on the pack horses. Baker, turning in the saddle watched intently.

Standing by the horses, Buck took a long look back the way they had come. Blackness covered most of the landscape, with the faint moonlight making the sky only a little bit lighter. Other than the soft stamping of one of the horses, the night was silent.

'What's your interest in all this?' Baker asked quietly.

Buck chuckled softly. 'My ma always said I'd get in trouble, never being able to tell someone no when they asked for a favour. As far as this little trip is concerned, I don't have an interest. Oh, other than to help out where I can. Your sheriff seems like a good man, and I really wasn't doing anything else tonight.'

'Sheriff Brickey said you're in town to try to find out what happened to Lewis Clement. Are you friends of that family?'

'Nope. Friend of a friend, I guess you'd say. And that friend asked me, if I happened to be riding this way, would I do what I could.' Once again he laughed faintly. 'Just can't seem to get away from doing favours for people, I reckon.'

Shaking his head a little, Baker reined his horse around and headed off the ridge, down into the inky darkness. The moon, having dropped behind a mountain range further on, no longer helped. Finding a wide place in the trail, the two men stopped to wait for sunrise.

For a while they sat on their heels, holding the ends of the reins. Buck shook out a small quantity of tobacco into a slip of paper and deftly rolled a quirly. Striking a match against a rock, he lit the cigarette. Cool air rising from the depths of the canyon they were riding down into sent a chill through the men.

'Hope those fellas in the wagons are making it all right,' he said after a while.

'They should be OK. Even if the outlaws somehow

find out about the shipment, they aren't likely to hit them until daylight.'

'Any way of guessing who that gang might have in town to keep an eye on things?'

'No. We went over it a dozen times after the second robbery. There's a lot of men coming and going so it's impossible to tell who it could be. When the first shipment was taken, Sheriff Brickey sent someone down to Durango and sent out telegrams to banks to be on the lookout for anyone with a coupla pounds of gold. The bars are all stamped with the mark of the mine the metal came from so they'll be easily identified.'

'That wouldn't stop someone from melting the bars down, though.'

'Well, no. But it would certainly be suspicious if that someone came riding in wanting to trade that much gold for cash money. Especially after all the banks within a hundred miles or more have been notified.'

Buck pinched out the burning end of his smoke and noticed it was getting light. He was able to see a ways down the slope they were on, although the bottom was still hidden from view.

'Think it's light enough to ride on?' he asked, standing up and settling his gunbelt in place.

Baker didn't answer, but tightening the cinches, swung into the saddle. Buck smiled and wondered silently how long it would be before the man relaxed and trusted him.

By the time they reached level ground, the pre-dawn sky had lightened and they could make out the

116

trail as it twisted and turned along the canyon floor. A creek gurgled as it meandered around a boulder-strewn bottom. There were places, mostly dark, deep holes that Buck thought might be good fishing. Probably full of big lunkers just waiting for his hook. Glancing to one side as the first rays of the morning sun came over the eastern ridge, he saw up on the rock face evidence that at one time or another water had scoured the canyon wall. This would not be a good place to be caught during a run-off flooding, he knew.

Late in the morning, long after leaving the narrow confines of the canyon and riding across a wide flat sagebrush-eovered prairie, Baker angled off the trail toward a clump of tall cottonwood trees.

'That's were we come up to the San Juan River again,' he called back. 'There's a campsite over there. A good place to let the horses rest a bit and fix ourselves a meal.'

While Baker gathered a pile of firewood and got a small fire going, Buck stripped the gear off all the horses and let them roll in the dust.

With the last of the coffee poured over the fire, and the packs once more in place, the two men headed out. Late in the afternoon, with the sun about an hour from falling behind the mountains, Baker pulled up and looked back over his shoulder at Buck.

'I'd say we're another hour, maybe two from Durango,' he said, waving a hand in the direction they had been travelling. 'Our horses aren't that tired, but if you've a mind to, we could stop for the night. As I recall, there's a small pond over that way we could camp by and get a fresh start in the morning.'

Buck cuffed back his hat and, standing tall in the stirrups, took a long look all around. 'Well, far as I'm concerned, we might as well ride on in. There may be water over yonder, but it looks to me like the ground doesn't get any softer over there. Sleeping in a hotel bed tonight will feel a lot better.'

Baker settled back in the saddle and nodded. Touching his heel to his horse's side, he led out.

Durango, Buck could see as they crossed a bridge over the river and rode into town, was quite a bit bigger than Silverton, spread out along a pair of narrow gauge railroad tracks that ran down the middle of the main street. Most of the buildings lining each side of the street were mostly one and two-storey brick structures with a couple of single wooden plank-sided buildings mixed in.

'Durango's mayor is trying to pass a law that all buildings have to be brick. There was a fire a few years ago that nearly destroyed the town. The Durango bank is over there,' Baker said, pointing to the far side. 'This late, there's likely not to be anyone there. I think the best thing to do is ride on down to the marshal's office. He can send someone to unlock the vault so we can get rid of this gold.'

The jail and marshal's office was one of the two-storey buildings further down the street. Stopping at the hitching post in front, Buck swung gratefully out of the saddle and stretched his legs and back, feeling a twinge when the skin on his back pulled at the near-healed wound. Baker, after dropping his reins over the porch railing, pushed open the office door and disappeared inside.

Dusk had settled in while the pair were still out of town and now nearly everything in town was dark. On down the street, he could see light streaming out of two large windows, flooding the boardwalk. That was likely a saloon, Buck thought. Once the gold was safely stored away, he would offer to buy the first round of drinks.

The office door swung open and Baker came out followed by a short, bandy-legged older man. 'Buck, this is Marshal Gouch. He's sent someone for the bank manager. If you want to go ahead, we can protect the gold from here on.'

Buck smiled and nodded at the lawman. 'Evening, Marshal,' he said, touching the brim of his Stetson. 'My saddle partner here still isn't sure how far he can trust me,' he said, taking any sting out of his words by chuckling. 'Well, that's to be expected, I reckon. I see some lights down there a ways. What say you and the marshal come on down when you get your gold all locked up and I'll buy you both a drink. I expect we'll be able to get a bite to eat there, too.'

Not waiting for a response, he handed the pack horses' lead rope to the marshal and climbed back into the saddle.

The saloon was next door to the Strater Hotel, so before going through the swinging doors, Buck went in to sign the register. No matter what, he was going to sleep in a bed tonight.

After leaving the black horse out back in the

hotel's stable, all brushed down and fed a bait of grain, Buck headed for the saloon.

Finding a place at the long bar, he made quick work of his first glass of beer and ordered another. Asking about getting a dinner, the bartender told him the restaurant was closed.

'There's a large plate of sliced meat and cheese laid out at the other end of the bar, though,' the mustachioed barkeep said, waving in that direction. 'Restaurant closes early since the cook got married. Says her husband wants her home cooking his dinner. I suppose that means we'll be looking for a new cook before long. Anyway, help yourself to the plate of food down there.'

Nodding, Buck did just that. Finding a place within arm's length from the plate, he settled in.

'I'll bet you're here looking for work,' a man standing next to him said softly. 'You got the look of the kind of man they was looking for recently.'

Buck glanced over to make sure the old-timer was talking to him. 'Yeah,' the old man said, looking up at the tall cowboy, 'I know someone on the dodge when I see one. I might not look it, but I once rode the back trails myself.'

Trying to guess what the crusty old man was talking about, Buck looked down at his new friend. Standing about a foot shorter than Buck's six-foot height, his weather-wrinkled face had all the creases and folds of a hard life. Long moustaches covered his upper lip and hung in thin streams below his bristly chin. Straggly hair hung almost to his thin shoulders which were covered with a threadbare wool coat that had once been black but was now faded to blotchy browns. One pale, washed-out grey eye tracked at a wide angle from the other, making it difficult to tell exactly what the old coot was looking at.

This man may have once been a tough one, Buck thought, but not in the last twenty years or more. Glancing at his own reflection in the mirror behind the back bar, he silently agreed, though. The man looking back at him did have the look of a long rider. That trip down from Silverton had layered him with dust and made his own tired eyes look sunken in their sockets. Unless he got a bath and a shave some-where, it would be a wonder that the bow-legged marshal didn't lock him up just on suspicion.

'I wouldn't say anything,' the old man continued, as if Buck was who he thought he was, 'but I remem-ber seeing you one time, riding alongside that outlaw, Dutch Voles. I knew it was you the minute you walked in here.' Before Buck could say anything, his neighbour took a quick look around and then, keep-ing his voice low, went on, 'And I know why you're here. But you're a mite late.'

Buck almost laughed, but decided to keep a poker face. 'Now why am I late?' he asked, keeping he eye on the old man.

'Cos Voles left town almost a month ago. Headed north, he did. And with most of his gang, too. I figured they'd all gone and got hanged, over there in Ophir, but there he was, riding into town just like he didn't have a worry in the world. Waal, I'll tell you, I took a second look just to make sure it was him. Yep, it sure enough was.' The old man laughed and took

121

another sip of beer. 'I 'spect those vigilantes thought they got 'em all, but nossir, there they were. A good handful of that bunch what used to ride the owlhoot trail back before he took over the gang. That'd be about when I seen you riding with 'em. I wonder who all those fellas were that the vigilantes hanged? Anyhow, if you're looking for Voles, you'll have to ride some north. Don't know what it's all about, but that's the direction they all went.'

Buck held it in, trying not to laugh. Noticing how the old-timer put his empty beer glass down on the counter close by Buck's glass, it all made sense. The old man was making talk to get a free drink.

'Here, let me get you a beer,' he said, thinking the cost of a beer was worth being entertained with the tall story. Signalling to the bartender, he held up two fingers.

'Oh, oh,' his sidekick muttered quietly and moved a few feet away, 'here comes that damn marshal. Don't take offence, but I don't wanna be seen talking to ya.'

After paying for the beer, and picking up a full glass, Buck turned to see Baker and the Durango lawman coming down to stand beside him.

'Well, did you get everything taken care of, Baker?' he asked, motioning to the bartender again. 'Set these gentlemen up, will you.' Glancing around the room to see where the old man had disappeared too, he motioned to the platter of meat and cheese. 'Better get some of that, Baker. Seems that's all there is for supper. Something about the cook getting married. Now, there's something for people to think about, if they were thinking along those lines.' He laughed as Baker's face flushed.

'Yes, the bank manager came over and everything is safely locked up. And I guess I should apologize for my actions. We did get the shipment safely here. Your plan was a good one.'

'Mr Baker here told me how you worked it,' Marshal Gouch said, nodding his thanks for the drink when the bartender placed glasses of beer in front of the two men. 'I've been on the lookout for anyone with too much gold in their pockets but haven't seen anything yet. I did hear that one of the Ophir outlaws was spotted in town a few weeks ago. Man name of Dutch Voles. Said to have been part of the gang that the vigilantes up there was supposed to have hung out to dry.' Shaking his head, he frowned. 'Can't believe people sometimes, thinking they can simply go out and hang a bunch of men because they look like outlaws.'

Buck quickly looked around the crowded room, trying again to spot the old man who had been talking to him, but not seeing any sign of him. Maybe there was something in what he'd been talking about after all.

CHAPTER 14

The next morning, after a breakfast of ham, eggs and fried potatoes, Charlie Baker and Buck started the trip back to Silverton. The ride back went a lot easier for Buck after catching up on his sleep in the thick mattress on the hotel bed and both men rode a lot easier than on the ride down. Before they were much more than out of sight of Durango, they were on a first-name basis. The tension of carrying such a large quantity of gold bullion had disappeared with the locking of the treasure in the Durango bank. Even carrying a pair of leather saddle-bags filled with cash money, Charlie Baker was somehow more trusting of his saddle partner.

'We keep up the pace and you'll almost be back in Silverton in time for Mrs Ritter's supper at the boarding-house,' Charlie commented at one point.

'Riding the wagon road is cutting off a lot of travel,' Buck said, reaching out to pat the sweaty neck of the black horse. 'This is the hardest my horse has had to work in quite a while. Does him good, but he won't be worth beans for a day or two.'

'I figure we rode more'n seventy-five miles taking the backcountry trail. Putting that many miles on these animals is asking a lot.'

'Yeah, but they're both holding up pretty good.'

Stopping only to give the horses a breather and not making a noon halt, the two rode into Silverton just as darkness came over the town. Too late for supper at the boarding-house, Buck figured he could miss a meal without doing any damage. Baker decided he'd store the saddle-bag full of bank notes in the mill office safe overnight. With no more than a wave and a quiet 'goodnight' the pair separated and went their own way.

Buck took the time to brush down the black horse's sweat-crusted hide after stripping off the saddle gear. Peeling off his shirt he ducked his upper body in a bucket of cold well water and used the shirt to dry off. Making sure the black had water and a scoop of oats, he filled the manger with fresh hay and, giving the animal a last slap on the muscled rump, walked around to the front of Mrs Ritter's house.

Stepping quietly so not to bother any of the other guests, he climbed the stairs to his room and piled into bed.

Washing up and putting on his last clean shirt, Buck was the last one down for breakfast the next morning. As usual, talk was sparse as the platters of hotcakes, fried eggs and ham slices made the rounds. Buck was pouring himself a second cup of coffee when he caught on that he was being studied. Not letting on, he watched as he sipped the hot brew and discovered that nearly every other guest was watching him closely.

Nobody said anything as having finished their meal, each nodded to Mrs Ritter and went about their business. With only the landlady and Buck left in the room, she looked directly at the tall man.

'I don't want any trouble brought into the house,' she said sternly. 'Whatever you've been up to, keep it away from here. You're paying for a place to sleep and the meals and that's all.'

Buck put his empty cup down and smiled. 'Well, whatever's on everybody's mind is beyond me. But I'll not be causing you any trouble.'

Nodding abruptly, the woman rose and without another word went out of the room, heading toward the kitchen.

Stepping outside, he stopped long enough to settle his Stetson and decided to go talk to the sheriff. Somehow he was going to have to come up with a way to let Miss Clement know he had not been able to find out anything about her brother. Professor Fish was another bridge to cross. He'd have to be assured that everything had been done that could be done.

Already the water wagons had been busy wetting down the main street and the first of the ore wagons had already taken their first loads of the day to the stamp mill. Stepping carefully, Buck tried to keep his boots from picking up the gummy mess.

'Well, I see you two made it back,' Sheriff Brickey greeted Buck, when the tall cowboy pushed open the office door. 'No problem was there?' he asked, motioning the other man to take a chair. 'Coffee's hot,' he added.

'Thanks,' Buck said, pouring a cup and settling himself in one of the office chairs. 'No, no problems. Other than a long time in the saddle it was no more than a long ride. We didn't run into any trouble or even see anyone until we got to Durango. What happened with the wagons?'

'Whose slick idea was that, to let both wagons go out with nothing but boxes of rocks?'

'Oh, it was just something Charlie and I came up with at the last moment.'

'Well, it seemed to have worked. Nobody knows how they found out, but the bandits did. The hold-up gang stopped *both* wagons. Clevis Smothers was with the wagon that took the main road south and after the outlaws broke open one of the boxes, he says they didn't waste any time. Just took off hell-for-leather. Clevis and the guards just turned around and came back to town. Got in a bit after daylight.'

'And the other wagon was stopped too? Anyone hurt?'

Brickey chuckled. 'No, but the men riding guard on that one said one of the outlaws started cussing enough to turn the air blue. They smashed all the boxes before riding away. They brought the wagon back and got here a mite after noon.'

'Wonder who's behind getting the word out to that gang,' Buck mused.

'Now that is a good question. There's one man in town seems to think you had something to do with it.' Sheriff Brickey sat back and watched Buck's face.

'Someone thinks I'm involved with the hold-up gang?' Buck glanced back toward the jail cells. 'Has your jailer been mouthing off again?'

'Nope. Well, only a little. But it isn't old John who's talking it up that your coming to town when you did was a little suspicious.'

Buck took a sip from his steaming cup and frowned, thinking back to the old coot he'd bought a beer for in the saloon in Durango. 'Ever hear of someone named Dutch Voles?'

Brickey nodded. 'Yeah. He was thought to be the leader of the gang that was hitting the mines over at Ophir. Some say the vigilantes got him, others say he got clean away. Why? How'd his name come up?'

Quickly Buck told the lawman about being mistaken for one of Voles's gang. 'I got to admit, I looked mighty rough that night, but so far as I know, I've never been part of any gang of bad men.'

Brickey chuckled. 'No, I didn't think you were. Anyway, I knew where you were and those men who're talking against you don't.' Pushing himself away from the desk, the sheriff stood up. 'Finish that coffee and let's go see what Brass Kingston has to say.'

'Is he the one doing the talking?'

'Yeah. Yesterday evening, over at the Gold Dust Saloon. Just innocently asking the questions, wondering about you and wondering where you had gotten off to.'

Shutting the office door behind them, the two men headed down the street toward the bank, reaching the corner building just as Charlie Baker came around the corner.

'Hey, there, Sheriff. I heard about the wagons being stopped. Buck's plan to take the gold by pack horse worked out pretty good.'

Brickey shot a glance at the tall man beside him. 'Uh huh. Makes me wonder what kind of trick he'll come up with next time.'

Buck chuckled. 'Oh, there won't be any next time as far as I'm concerned. I'll be long gone from here when the next shipment is sent south. You'll have to come up with your own deception.'

'You heading in to see Kingston?' Brickey asked Baker.

'Yeah. I thought he'd want to know that the gold is safe and that Burton and Howard have the cash money to pay their miners.'

'As one of the miners' association, I guess he should be told,' Sheriff Brickey nodded, 'but do you mind if you don't tell him right away? Kinda let the conversation get started first?'

'Well, OK,' said Baker, hesitantly. 'What's this all about?'

Brickey smiled. 'You'll see. Come on,' he said, pushing through the door to the bank.

The three men had no more than got into the room when Brass Kingston came hurrying out of his office. 'Sheriff, I was just coming over to talk to you. I've got some concerns about this man here, Armstrong, that you should hear about.'

Buck stopped and waited.

'So I've heard,' Brickey said. 'Seems there's some talk going around that Mr Armstrong here is part of the gang of men holding up the gold shipments. What's that all about?'

'Yes, Sheriff. A number of the local businessmen were in the Gold Dust yesterday after supper, talking about how the hold-up gang learned about when the shipments were going out. Someone pointed out that the only stranger in town was this man right here, Armstrong. And when they learned about there being two wagons going out, with the gold only in one, Armstrong was the only stranger who knew about it. I, and most of the others, think that points the finger at him. We want you to arrest him.'

Sheriff Brickey looked long and hard, first at Buck, then turning his head, at Charlie Baker before turning back to the banker.

Buck noticed that while Kingston's thumbs were hooked in the armholes of his vest, the two bank clerks were standing in their cages. In the hands of one he could see the blued steel barrels of a revolver.

'That's an interesting claim to make, Brass,' Brickey said slowly. 'Let's see. The only men who knew of the plan to send out a fake shipment in one wagon were Howard, Burton, Charlie, here, and Buck. Oh, and you.'

'And he's the only stranger,' Kingston broke in, pointing a finger at Buck.

The sheriff nodded. 'That's true. But there's a problem with your thinking, Brass. The hold-up gang didn't get anything in either wagon because Charlie and Buck had loaded the gold on to a coupla pack horses. They took the old Indian trail down to Durango. Made it safely down with the gold and back with enough cash money for the miners to get paid. Now, somehow that shoots a hole in your claim, doesn't it?'

Kingston's face slowly turned red as he heard what the sheriff was saying.

'You know,' Buck said softly, 'most anyone making talk like that could find themselves in trouble with me. I don't like it much when someone calls me an outlaw.'

Kingston's mouth worked as he tried to find the right words. 'Well, maybe we were a little hasty. But you do understand, losing the first couple of shipments hurt us all,' he said, his speech picking up steam as he explained. 'Without the miners getting paid, every business in town loses out. We all count on that payroll and, I guess, it's got us worried. You understand, don't you?'

'Yep. I do,' Buck said, thumbing the thong from the hammer of his holstered Colt. 'But if I were to be accused of something like that, it might make me a little angry.' Lifting his six-gun a bit and letting it drop back, he let his face harden. 'And a man can't let something like that just go by without standing up, now can he? You do understand, don't you?'

The banker's face paled as he watched Buck playing with his revolver. 'Yes, I do understand,' he stammered. 'And I am sure all of us will apologize for that thoughtless talk. I'll make sure everybody learns that we were close to making a mistake.'

Baker coughed softly. 'Well, now that we've got that out of the way, back to business. That's what I came by to tell you, Brass. The miners will be getting paid later today, so business should be back to normal in town once again.'

For a long moment Buck stared coldly into Kingston's eyes and then, nodding once, abruptly turned and walked out of the bank.

Crossing the muddy street once again, Buck took one of the rocking chairs on the hotel porch and watched as Charlie Baker and Sheriff Brickey came out of the bank. For a few minutes they stood on the walk in front of the two-storey building talking. Noticing Buck, they crossed over, dodging an empty ore wagon going in one direction and nearly getting hit by a full one heading for the stamping mill.

'Someone is going to have to do something about those wagons,' Brickey grumped, stamping the mud from his boots as he climbed up the steps on to the porch.

'There's been some talk about cutting a new road around town,' Baker said, using a stick to dig a thick clump from first one low-heeled boot and then the other. Both men sat back against the porch railing as they tried to clean their footwear.

'Your friend Kingston is fighting it, Buck. Seems he likes the idea of there being a lot of wagon traffic through town, makes everything look busier, he says.'

Buck unfolded from the chair and leaned against a porch upright between the two men, watching the traffic in the street and didn't respond.

'Oh,' Sheriff Brickey said jokingly, 'I don't know if Brass Kingston likes anyone who isn't from the local business community. Those folks make up the crowd that believes everything he says. It'll be interesting to see how he gets them to stop talking about Buck being one of the outlaw gang.'

'Your banking friend,' Buck murmured, 'may have other things to think about soon.'

'What's that?' Brickey asked, still in a light-hearted way.

'Well, it looks a lot like he's about to have some real interesting visitors.' Both men looked around to see what Buck was watching.

'Those two men,' the tall man said softly, nodding toward the bank, 'there at the bank's hitching rail, just rode in and climbed down from their horses. When those other four rode in, they handed their reins to the first two. Now what does that look like to you?'

Brickey watched as four of the men, one with a feed sack thrown over a shoulder, stepped up from the mud on to the boardwalk and then pushed through the door into the bank.

'Will you look at that?' Baker said quietly, 'Gentlemen, we've got front row seats to a bank robbery.'

CHAPTER 15

'I suppose we ought to do something about it,' Sheriff Brickey said. 'After all that's my job.'

'I'll go this way,' Buck said, and moved down the walk until he was hidden behind an ore wagon coming down the street. Baker, slipping a revolver from under his coat, went the other way, crossing behind another wagon. The sheriff turned into the hotel and asked the clerk if he still had his rifle behind the counter.

'Why, yes, Sheriff,' the thin-faced young man said, surprised at the question. 'You need it?'

'Yeah. Loaded?' At the clerk's nod, the lawman smiled. 'How about I borrow it a minute.'

The carbine handed to Brickey was a Henry, a carry over from the Civil War. Levering a .44 calibre cartridge into the breech, Brickey smiled. He now had fourteen shots to use against the robbers. Using the same post Buck had been leaning against, he sighted across at the horse-holders.

Where the sheriff and Baker were, Buck didn't know. He wasn't even thinking about them as he edged around the back of an oncoming empty wagon and stopped. Holding his Colt down beside his leg he waited for the ball to open.

A shot fired from inside the bank was the starting gun. Seconds later men rushed out of the building and started down the steps only to be halted when rifle fire opened up at them from across the street. When one of the men by the horses pulled his pistol, Buck fired, dropping the man.

'We quit,' came a yell from one of the hold-up men, throwing his hands in the air. 'Don't shoot any more, I quit.' Buck saw only two men standing, backed up against their frightened horses, both with empty hands high above their heads.

'A couple of them went back into the bank,' Brickey called. Before anyone could move, more gunshots were heard from inside.

Silence fell like a blanket over the town. Even the ore wagons on the street, both loaded and empty, stood with their drivers nowhere to be seen.

From each direction, Charlie Baker and Buck made their way up on the boardwalk and started toward the bank's open door.

Keeping close to the wall, Buck took a quick look around and into the bank. Two men lay on the floor, one flat on his back, his eyes staring unseeing at the pressed tin ceiling. The other looked at first like he was sitting on the floor with his back against a wall. The blood-splattered front of his shirt showed he wasn't sleeping.

'We shot them,' a trembling voice called out weakly from across the room.

Buck stepped in followed by Sheriff Brickey.

'Well, well,' the lawman muttered, kicking at the feed sack that was clutched in the hand of one of the dead robbers. The sack had burst and a few gold bars were scattered across the floor.

'Hey,' Charlie Baker said, when he came in and saw the bars, 'those have our marks on them. This is some of the gold that was taken in the first shipment that was hit. How in the hell did they get here?'

For a moment nobody said anything, then one of the clerks came out from behind the counter, still holding a big, heavy, double-action Starr revolver in one hand.

'They came in and before we could do anything, pointed their guns at us. That one' – he pointed the Starr – 'went into Mr Kingston's office and the other just stared at us. There was a shot and he came out carrying that bag. Henry and I were thankful they left without shooting us when all hell broke loose outside and those two came running back in. I didn't even think. I just shot them. Oh, Gawd, I killed them.'

Brickey nodded. 'So that's the story. Kingston had the gold in his safe and these outlaws came in to get it. You know,' he said, glancing over at Baker, 'I would go so far as to say we now know who the spy was, letting the gang know when the shipments were going out. Those two outside who gave up will likely fill us in on how that worked.'

Buck, standing near the door, slowly replaced the spent cartridges in his Colt. He hadn't been aware of it, but he had fired all six shots in the brief fight out front. Shaking his head, he pushed through the crowd that filled the door to get outside.

Thinking about Kingston, Buck let his eyes travel down the muddy street. The ore wagons were once again on the move and someone, far too late for all the excitement, was coming into town, pushing his horse to a lather. Buck watched, wondering about the rider and speculating on what would cause someone to be in such a big hurry. If anything, he thought, it would be one of the bank robbers trying to get away, except he was going in the wrong direction. But, counting the two dead men in the bank, all six were accounted for. Leaning against a porch upright again, he watched the oncoming rider, swerving to go around a slower wagon.

'Mr Armstrong.' The rider was Elizabeth Montague. 'Mr Armstrong,' she was calling as she pulled up her horse and jumped out of the saddle. 'Have you seen the sheriff? I must find him.'

'Why yes, he's in the bank.' Buck motioned with a thumb over his shoulder. 'What's the trouble?'

'Those cattlemen are bunching a herd down by our furthest fence. Father sent me in to find Sheriff Brickey,' she explained breathlessly, coming up the steps and running into the bank. Buck followed right behind.

'Sheriff, we need your help,' he heard the girl tell the lawman. Charlie Baker had been crouched over piling up the bars of gold but when he heard her speak, he stood right up. Anyone watching could tell from the way they looked at each other that there was something more than a Saturday night dance between them. 'Hello, Charlie,' she added, smiling a little.

Then, remembering why she was in town, she turned back to Sheriff Brickey. 'Those riders from Crown have a herd down by our southern fences. We need you to come out and stop them. Father thinks they'll push through sometime after dark.'

'Miss Montague, I can't help you. My jurisdiction, such as it is, is only for the town. These are the people who pay me to keep the law. Anything outside is taken care of by the army or the State Marshal's office down in the capitol. Anyway, I've got this bank robbery to clean up. I'm sorry, but . . .' He stopped, holding his hands up. It was obvious he wasn't happy about it.

The girl's shoulders slumped. Frowning, Buck spoke up. 'Well, I guess it wouldn't hurt for me to ride out to your pa's place for a visit. I don't have a badge, but I can get mighty testy at times.'

'Oh, Mr Armstrong, thank you. I just don't know what'll happen if those riders push their cattle into our fields. All we've got to try to stop them is Father and Mr Balsom and a few of our hired hands. Would you come and see what you can do?'

'Buck,' Sheriff Brickey said, shaking his head, 'you could be getting into something you'll find hard to get out of. The trouble Montague and Balsom are having with Ludel can't be solved with guns. It'll have to be taken to the territorial government.'

Elizabeth frowned. 'I wouldn't want you to get hurt, Mr Armstrong. Father and the others will have to fight, but that's because it's our farms that are at stake.'

'And as I recall,' he said, smiling first down at her

and then over at the sheriff, 'it was you and your mother who likely saved my life, at your farm. Anyway, I'll just go along for a little visit. Sheriff, my black horse is still resting up from the big ride to Durango. What say I borrow one of those horses the hold-up men were riding?'

'I doubt anyone'll argue with that. But ride carefully. As you just mentioned, someone has already tried to back shoot you once. It could have been one of the Crown riders.'

'Could have, but just as likely not. And thinking about it, we'd better take two horses. Miss Montague was pushing her pony pretty hard.'

'Yeah. Leave hers tied at the railing and I'll have someone take it over to the stable after a while.'

'C'mon, Miss Montague. Let's go see what we can do.'

'Elizabeth?' Baker said, stepping over to take her hand. 'I'd ride out to help, but' – and he waved one hand behind him – 'I can't just leave now. You do understand, don't you?'

'I suppose, Charlie,' her voice was soft and for his ears only. 'But the people here in town seem to forget that we're a part of things, too. The law isn't just for those who live along that muddy Main Street. Father thinks everyone in the valley has to pull together; or we'll never be a community and I feel the same way.'

Taking her hands away from his she turned. 'Come on, Mr Armstrong. Let's go see what a few people who don't live in town can do.'

Buck almost broke out laughing at the look on

Baker's face, but turned away before the mill owner could see it.

Taking a quick look at the horses tied to the hitching rail, Buck chose two and handed the reins of one, a strong-looking bay, to Elizabeth. 'You were pretty hard on him, don't you think?'

'Yes, but I'm tired of being a part of the farm, separate from the people who live here in town.' He held the bay while she swung up into the saddle. 'Oh, beans,' she exclaimed. 'Never mind. When this is all over, he'll apologize and I'll be contrite and we'll be OK. I do like him a lot, but sometimes, well, sometimes I just despair.'

Chuckling to himself, Buck climbed up and into a well-used saddle. The horse he'd selected was pale yellowish buckskin. All of the outlaws' horses had looked like high-priced stock and the decision of which to take was easy; any of them would run circles around most available horses over at the stable. Except for his own black stud, that is. Having quality horseflesh under you when trying to escape was important to any desperado and this gang was no different. He wondered who would end up owning the horses once everything settled down. If it ever did.

It was late afternoon when they rode into the Montague front yard. Luke Balsom and Eli Montague were sitting on the front porch talking when Elizabeth and Buck stepped down.

'I couldn't get the sheriff to come out, Father,' Elizabeth said, 'but Buck, uh, Mr Armstrong here, said he'd come see what could be done.'

'Well, that's about what I expected from our local law,' Montague grumbled, coming down to shake Buck's hand. 'Mister Armstrong, I want to thank you for bringing my daughter back out. Sending her in alone wasn't exactly my idea, but she wouldn't wait.' Motioning him to come up and take a chair, he went on, 'I don't want to sound ungrateful, but what can any of us do? I thought Ludel and his men would back off if there was a badge standing in his way.'

'Yeah, I suppose it might help if a lawman was here. But then again, maybe not. I was raised on a cattle ranch down in Texas. Cowboys like to harass farmers, or anyone, for that matter. They outnumber you and can easily bring it to you. After all, you've both got women and your homes to protect. But what would happen if I were to step in? I have nothing to lose and, being one man, could move around faster. By the way, what happened to the cattle the last time a herd was pushed into your fields?'

'A bunch of Crown riders came in the next morning and herded them out. Didn't bother fixing the fences they'd cut the night before, either.'

Buck chuckled. 'That sounds like cattlemen. Have either of you got a good-sized corral anywhere on your farms?'

'Well, yes, we both have,' Balsom said, glancing at Montague. 'Big enough to hold our few head of milk stock and what horses and mules we have. Why?'

'If it was me, I'd make sure any cattle that I found in my crops would end up in my corral. The rancher could then pay for the damage, or I'd be offering the beef for sale to the town butcher.'

Balsom shook his head. 'That wouldn't stop those cowboys. All it'd do is get one of us killed.'

'Now, that's where I come in. Somehow I don't think I'd be so easy to shoot. Not,' he chuckled again, 'unless it was in the back.'

CHAPTER 16

One thing about farm living was the size of the meals coming out of the kitchen. Mrs Montague did her family, and this day guests, well. The platters of fried chicken, hot corn on the cob, fried green tomatoes, mashed potatoes and two large bowls of rich gravy next to platters of baking soda biscuits was more than filling. Strong, hot, black coffee and two of the thickest apple pies Buck had ever seen finished supper that evening. Groaning a little from the big meal, Buck felt like a waddling duck when, just at dusk, he pulled himself into the buckskin's saddle.

'I don't understand what you're planning to do, Buck.' Balsom and Montague had followed him out but stayed on the porch. 'Wouldn't it be better if there were more of us out there facing them? It seems foolhardy for you to be going alone.'

'We've talked this far enough. If I don't have to worry about where I throw my shots I can be more successful. Look, gentlemen, your hands are used to holding plough handles and my Colt and this Henry hanging off this saddle fit my hands. It'll be dark soon and that makes it even better. Now, go back inside and be ready to protect your families. If you hear a bunch of riders coming in, you'll know they got past me. Shoot as if you meant it.' He chuckled a little. 'But if you hear just one rider, I'd appreciate it if you didn't be so quick to shoot. It just might be me.' Still laughing, he reined away.

From the directions given by Eli, Buck followed the outer fence line south, riding around a large field of ripening wheat. Far out of sight of the home place in the rolling flatland and beyond the triple strand of barbed wire he spotted a herd being loosely held. Leaving the buckskin behind, he climbed the fence and ambled through the sagebrush to get a closer look.

Counting four riders, two sitting their horses off to either side of the bunch and two relaxing by a small fire, he did a quick tally of the beeves. The forty or so head, mostly older range stock, were settled and moving normally while grazing on the sparse wild grasses. It wouldn't take much to get them moving into the field, Buck figured, once the fence was cut. If they hit the fence line at a lumbering run, it was likely the animals would be pretty well spread out before they calmed down and went back to feeding. Clearing the wheat field would mean doing a lot more damage.

Walking back to the buckskin, he pulled the Henry from the saddle scabbard and quickly checked it over. Well oiled and the tube under the barrel filled with .44 cartridges, he smiled. Let 'em come; he was ready. Settling back on his heels Buck rolled a smoke and, shielding the flame with his hat, waited for something to happen.

The loud spring of a tight fence wire being cut woke Buck from his slumber. Glancing at the sky, he saw he'd been dozing about an hour. Full darkness had fallen and the moon hadn't yet come over the far mountains. Levering a shell into the breech and leaving his horse behind him, Buck trotted along the fence toward the sound of cowboys yelling and cattle being moved.

Hurrying as fast as he could without twisting an ankle in his high-heeled riding boots, he almost over ran the first Crown rider. The man was standing next to a fence post and still had a pair of wire cutters in one hand. He was turning to look over a shoulder when Buck swung the rifle, catching the man in the back of the head with the barrel.

Stopping, he brought the rifle up and fired twice over the heads of anyone near the small herd. He hoped the loud gunshots would give the riders second thoughts about moving the herd toward the fence. For a long moment, the yelling of the riders faded. Then, off to one side, someone fired a revolver in his direction.

Swinging the rifle that way, but keeping the barrel aimed higher than any mounted man, Buck quickly fired a couple of more shots. This time someone yelled. Buck thought he'd probably come too close for comfort to one of the cowboys. At the yell, another herder opened fire from behind where Buck figured the cattle were. Shifting that way he fired again before turning back toward the first shooter.

Even with all the shooting, most of it coming from in front of them, the cattle were being pushed at a run toward the fence. Jerking off his hat, he jumped toward the lead steers and, yelling at the top of his voice, swung the hat back and forth. The action caused the animals to swerve but a large enough section of fence had been cut that they were able to keep running.

Not wanting to shoot any of the riders or the cattle, Buck stopped short of running into the animals and was trying to think of what to do next when something crashed into the back of his head. Slammed to the ground, he was unconscious and didn't feel his attacker kick him.

'All I did was pay him back for cracking my skull.' Buck heard the complaint coming from a distance. Shaking his head to stop the roaring in his ears caused the dull throbbing behind his eyes to boom. At first he wasn't sure where he was. He knew his eyes were open but everything was black. Lying on his back, he slowly rolled over and with great effort, got up on his hands and knees. Resting there, he breathed deep. The air was thick with the smell of smoke. Afraid to move his head, he waited to see if his vision would come back.

'It's a good thing he's got a hard head, *amigo*. Señor Ludel was very clear about not killing anyone.' This voice, as the thick cotton filling Buck's head started to disappear, was familiar. The dull pounding ache brought a moan from deep in his throat.

'Ah, *mi amigo* is coming awake. I must see to him. You are a fortunate *caballero. Vaya, compadre,* before Señor Ludel changes his mind.' Buck heard, suddenly remembering, the speaker was Reynaldo, the Mexican who backed Crown's owner.

The noise of a bar being lifted from the door and a shaft of bright sunlight caused Buck to rear back, using his hands to cover his eyes.

'Ah, Señor Armstrong. It is so good to be alive this fine morning, no?' the tall, thin man said, chuckling. 'But without a doubt, your head is sore, *verdad?* The *vaquero* who struck you wishes me to tell you how sorry he is. It was all a little mistake.'

'The hell it was,' Buck growled, his throat raspy and dry. 'Your men were stampeding cattle into the farmers' wheat. What's the point of that, anyway?'

'*Sí*, I agree, *señor*. It is not very neighbourly. But it is the orders of Señor Ludel, and I am but one who follows the orders of he who pays.' Reynaldo chuckled again. 'As you well know, eh? But let me get you some water, and maybe even some food. You will feel better when you have tortillas and beans in your stomach. Wait here and I will be back.'

Shutting the door behind him, Buck heard the bar drop in place. Blackness once again filled the room. Moving with some effort, he stood and, weaving a little, took the two steps to the door and pushed, feeling a twinge of pain in his almost healed shoulder. The door was firmly closed.

Using his hand to feel along the wall, he shuffled to one side and sat down. Until his head cleared, and he could see where he was, there was nothing to do.

147

Buck had his eyes closed when the door was opened again. Using one hand to shade them, he looked around the room he was in. He expected to find himself in a storeroom in a barn. Instead, he saw he was in a small, square, dirt-floored log building. From the cloth-wrapped bundles hanging from the rafters he knew he was being held prisoner in a smokehouse. Reynaldo, keeping his right hand free and his eyes on Buck, placed a cloth-covered platter on the floor just inside the door and reached back for a water jug.

'It isn't much, but until Señor Ludel decides what happens with you, it will have to do.'

'So I'm to be kept prisoner?'

'*Sí.* It is a problem for Señor Ludel. He doesn't want to have anyone killed, or even hurt too badly, but what to do with you? He doesn't know.'

'You wouldn't have any trouble figuring that out, would you.' It wasn't a question.

Reynaldo chuckled. 'No, *señor.* For me it is easy.'

'Tell me,' Buck asked, after taking a drink of water from the jug, 'what's the old man after, running his cattle into the farmers' fields?'

Reynaldo leaned a shoulder against the door jamb. 'Oh, that is a craziness, no? Ever since he married Señora Nell, he has not been himself. He was a good man to work for, and Crown is a good spread. Lots of land up on the ridges for summer feed and enough land down here on the flats protected from the winter storms to carry over the stock. But all of a sudden he tells me, Reynaldo, chase those sodbusters out. I argue. He says either I do it or he finds a new *segundo* and he gets it done. So I do it. *Qué mas?*'

Buck reached over and lifted the cloth. A pile of flat tortillas sat next to a low bowl filled with a brown mixture.

'It is beans and beef. Very good. Señor Ludel is from Texas and has a Mexican cook.'

'And what's the story with his young wife?' Buck asked, using a tortilla to scoop up some of the food and then, after taking a bite, reaching for the water bottle. 'Whooey, there's some spice in that, isn't there?'

Reynaldo laughed. '*Sí.* It is the chilli peppers that give it the flavour. Water won't stop the sting, but eat a little of the tortilla and it will go away.'

Buck did as he was told and found the burning fade away. Taking a small amount this time, he tried it again.

'The wife?' Reynaldo smiled. '*Sí*, she is *bonito*, very pretty, no? But she is too young for him, I think. He does not let her out of his sight. It is not a good thing.' Looking over his shoulder, he pushed away from the door and stepped back.

'Hey, Reynaldo,' Buck called out before the door could be closed, 'how about some light in here? No reason to keep me in the dark, is there?'

'I will open the vent. But keep in mind, there is always someone watching so don't do anything foolish. *Comprende?*'

'Yeah, I understand.'

The door closed and a few seconds later a piece of the roof was moved to one side. Looking up, Buck saw a thick mesh covered the opening, about two-foot square. Sitting back, he finished making a meal of the meat and bean mixture, all the while looking his prison cell over. The logs that made up the walls had been closely fitted and the spaces between them chinked with mud that had dried in place. Even if he could dig that chinking out, there wouldn't be enough room to make a difference. Getting up and inspecting the door, he could see that it had been fashioned to fit flush with the doorframe. As a smokehouse, it was well built.

With his stomach full and half a bottle of water left, he found his head had stopped throbbing. Sitting back down, he studied his predicament, trying to figure out his next move.

Time hung heavy and he had no way of telling how long it had been when he heard the bar being lifted from the door again. Not getting up, he wondered how he could go about getting Reynaldo to come into the small room. That thought went when he saw it was Nell Ludel standing with the door only partially open.

'Mr Armstrong,' she said urgently, 'I've only got a few minutes before someone will come looking for me. I need your help.'

'Well, Mrs Ludel, I don't think I'm in any position to help anyone. I can't even help myself.'

'If you will promise to help me, I will get you out of here. But you must promise.'

'Promise you what?'

'To help me get away. You must promise to take me to the railroad in Durango.'

Buck shook his head. 'I seem to recall a coupla other fellows doing just that, and not getting too far. Your husband and his hired hands were close to catching up with those two who were helping you the last time, weren't they?'

'Yes. But I think you're smarter than those two,' she said, glancing back over her shoulder before going on. 'I have something else to trade. But you have to promise me you'll help me.'

'What else do you have? I'm not someone like Hugo; I don't mess with any married woman.'

'Not that,' she said disgustedly. 'I can tell you what you want to know. I know what happened to that newspaper man, Lew Clement.'

CHAPTER 17

Buck was halted in his tracks and before he could react to her statement, she slammed the door closed, dropped the bar and ran off.

'Señora,' he heard Reynaldo's voice from outside the closed door, 'you must be more careful. And you, *señor*,' he called a little louder, 'if you are not also careful, *el jefe* will decide for me to shoot you. It should be clear that he does not like anyone to get too close to his woman. *Comprende?*' Buck didn't say anything.

Not doubting that she hadn't replaced the bar, or that Reynaldo didn't check it, Buck still had to push his weight against the door. It was as solid as ever. Tilting his head back to take a mouthful of water from the jug, he looked up at the opening in the roof.

Whoever had built this smokehouse had made the hole to act as a vent and had secured the mesh over it to keep out varmints. Buck wondered just how strong that mesh had been nailed down. Just sitting back and waiting until someone decided what to do about him didn't feel right. If Ludel got the notion, he was likely to tell the Mexican gunman to make sure the cowboy's body was never found. He had to do something and the opening looked like the best place to start.

A series of pole rafters had been laid across the tops of the log walls on which to hang the meat that was being smoked. Jumping up and grabbing one of those poles, Buck swung up and threw a leg over it. Pulling his body up stretched the shoulder injury again. Hoping the wound hadn't been torn open, he steadied himself and reached out to the frame that had been nailed around the hole. Pushing a hand against the screen, he felt it give a little but not enough. What he needed was a pry bar of some kind.

Sitting on the pole with his feet hanging, he looked around below him, trying to find something to work with. Nothing. There was nothing but the four walls and the half-dozen or so cloth-covered hunks of meat. Probably hams, he thought. Reaching down to touch one, he leaned too far and had to grab the thin rope that the meat was hanging by. Only it wasn't rope. Looking closely in the shadows, Buck saw that steel rods had been bent in to S-shapes, one end hooking around the pole and the other jabbed through the sacking. He had his bar to pry with.

Pulling himself up through the hole and then scrambling down and off the narrow shingled roof took only a minute or two. Reynaldo had warned that someone would be watching the smokehouse but nobody gave the alarm. Standing at a corner of his prison, he searched the yard and outbuildings but didn't see anyone. He was in the clear.

A huge barn was to his right and, stepping around to the other side, he saw the main house. Both buildings had been painted recently, the barn a dull red and the house white with bright red shutters on either side of its windows. The wide shaded veranda fronted the house. The door Buck was watching was around one side. A huge wooden water barrel stood next to the door. It was, he fugured, the kitchen door. Taking his time to think about which way to go, he was about to head for the barn when he heard a muffled gunshot from the main house.

Without another thought he dashed for the back door. The wooden door was open, a thin wire screen door keeping the flies out. From somewhere inside he heard loud voices. Slowly, and as quietly as he could, Buck opened the screen and stepped inside. Counters with crockery lined one wall and a huge, black, iron stove another. On one counter a tray sectioned by thin wood strips and lined with a waxy paper held eating utensils, knives, forks and spoons. Next to the tray was a collection of knives, each in a slit cut into a block. Buck took the largest, a worn wooden-handled butcher knife with an eight-inch blade. The argument from another room was louder.

'But I did it for you, Señora Nell,' he heard Reynaldo plead. 'I did everything for you.'

'They will never believe you,' Nell Ludel responded, almost emotionless as if she was explaining something to a child. 'I'll have to tell the sheriff that you shot him. I certainly wouldn't want them to think I did it, would I?'

'Tell the sheriff? *Por que?* We can be gone a long time before anybody comes into the house. Now you can do as you have wanted, you can go back to the city. And I will go with you.'

Buck got down on his hands and knees and from that low angle, peeked around a corner into the next room, a dining-room filled with a long, dark-wood table, fancy chairs lining both sides. The room was empty. Standing up, he moved across toward another door. The voices were closer now.

'Oh, I admit that's what I wanted,' the widow Ludel laughed softly. 'And there was always someone willing to help me, wasn't there? Even you, our faithful ranch foreman. Tell me, if that man out in the smokehouse hadn't killed Hugo and Big Carl, would you have?' Her laugh was louder. 'Of course you would. Rufus would have told you to, and you would do it.'

Reynaldo cursed. 'It was all for you. It made me very angry when you said you were going off with that newspaper man. He wasn't good enough for you. Señor Ludel was told that he was to meet you and take you to Durango. He told me to get rid of him and I did. But it was for you.'

'And how did poor old Rufus hear about Lew? You told him. After you left my loving husband beat me. While you were killing that young man, Mr Ludel was slapping me and hitting me.' Her voice grew hard, 'Mr Ludel. I was to call him Mr Ludel. And I was to wear the dresses he wanted me to wear. Those old things. He wouldn't take me to the city to buy new ones, pretty ones. No. It had to be those same ones over and over. Well, no more.'

'*Sí.* Now we can go to the big city and you can buy new dresses. You are free of him and we can go where we like.' Buck could hear the smile in Reynaldo's words.

'Go? Why should I go anywhere? No, I must mourn my dear dead husband. It will be expected of me.'

'But that is what you wanted,' the pleading sound was back in Reynaldo's voice. 'That's what we talked about. You and me, going together.'

Nell Ludel laughed. 'That was then. Things have changed. I am the widow of rancher Rufus Ludel. This is my ranch now.'

'But, *señora*, that is not what you said.'

'But it is what I'm saying now. I would never have gone off with you. Your prisoner, Armstrong said he would take me to the railroad.'

'You would not go with me?'

She laughed again. 'No. You are the foreman, or,' she hesitated, '*was* the ranch foreman. Of course you can't expect to stay here now. The sheriff from town will arrest you if you do. No, you'll have to run.'

'I can't do that. They will put on the telegraph my name. No, *señora*, you can not tell them I did this thing.'

'How will you stop me?'

Buck didn't like the change in Reynaldo's tone and thought it was about time to let them know he was there. Holding the butcher knife by the blade down along side his leg, he held up his left hand and stepped into the room, stopping abruptly. Lying at his feet with his arms outflung was Rufus Ludel's body. A six-gun lay in the dead man's curled fingers.

Reynaldo's revolver appeared in his hand almost like magic. 'Señor Armstrong,' he said after a minute, 'you surprise me. Tell me, how did you get out of the tiny smokehouse? Ah,' he went on, not giving Buck time to answer, 'Sí, I remember. You' – he moved to point the gun at Nell – 'let him get out. Ah, that was not wise, señora.'

Nell was looking at Buck with surprise. She glanced at Reynaldo, 'No, I made sure the bar was in place when you called me into the house,' she said. Then looking back at Buck. 'How did you get away?'

'Pure strength of character,' Buck said softly. 'But it looks as if I've missed all the excitement. How'd you come to shoot the old man, Reynaldo?'

'I was foolish, señor, very foolish. Señor Ludel was yelling at his wife and that was OK, but when he slapped her, that was not OK. I shot him. Foolish of me, I thought the señora there was waiting for my help so we could go away together. Now I learn that is not to be. So foolish, sí?'

Buck smiled and nodded. 'Oh, yes. You can always count on a woman to be contrary. Now, amigo, can I put my arm down?'

'Oh, sí. Be comfortable. Your strength of character got you out of the smokehouse but it did not hand you a pistol. I wonder why?'

'Reynaldo,' Nell Ludel cut in, 'here is your chance. You can shoot Armstrong and we'll tell the sheriff that he killed Rufus. Then you can ride on and I'll be free.'

Reynaldo stood holding his six-gun loosely, slowly shaking his head from one side to the other. 'Ah, *Madre de Dios*, the kind of woman you are,' he said sadly. 'To think I felt such a great desire for you.' Still shaking his head, he brought the barrel up and shot the woman.

As Reynaldo pulled the trigger, Buck's right aim flexed, bringing the butcher knife up and back. Whipping it forward he let go. The knife spun in the air, turning three complete cycles before burying the blade deep in the Mexican's chest.

Without stopping his motion, Buck crouched and picked up the six-gun from Ludel's hand. Thumbing back the hammer and not taking time to aim he shot Reynaldo. The Mexican was standing, looking with amazement at the knife handle sticking out of his shirtfront when the bullet struck him.

CHAPTER 18

Riding into the Montague front yard later in the day, Buck waited until Eli invited him to step down.

'Where did you get off to?' the farmer asked, surprise in his voice. 'Luke and I went out this morning and found that bunch of Crown cattle chomping up our young wheat but didn't see any sign of you. What happened?'

Buck gently touched the back of his head. 'I let one of Crown's riders get behind me. What did you do with the cattle?'

'Oh, we choused them out like we usually do. Patched up the fence and, well, I guess that's about all we can do.'

'I don't think you'll have any more trouble from Crown,' Buck said and quickly explained about the shooting. 'I wrapped Mrs Ludel in a blanket, but left the bodies on the floor like they were. I don't know what'll happen.'

Mrs Montague gasped at what she'd heard but when Buck finished, she turned and went back up on the veranda. 'Elizabeth,' she called.

'What are you going to do, Mother?' Eli Montague asked looking up at his wife.

'Why, we're going to do the neighbourly thing, of course. Elizabeth and I will go over and take care of that poor woman. You go get Luke and that big son of his and follow. You can dig the graves.' Turning to Buck, she continued giving orders. 'And you go inform Sheriff Brickey. He'll probably say there is nothing he can do, but there is. He can come witness things and then notify the governor's office. Someone will have to come take over the ranch until things get figured out. Now, go on. Don't just stand there.'

Riding the buckskin toward town, Buck thought it all out. He could now finish the job he'd come to do. Louise Clement would just have to mourn her brother without knowing where Reynaldo had buried the body.

Looking over his shoulder, he judged the time and smiled.

'Well, horse,' he slapped the horse's yellowish-grey shoulder, 'if you'll step it up a mite I could be in time for one of Mrs Ritter's suppers.'

The buckskin, just like the black stud, didn't bother to respond.